ALSO BY RODMAN PHILBRICK

Freak the Mighty
The Fire Pony
Max the Mighty
REM World
The Last Book in the Universe
The Young Man and the Sea
The Mostly True Adventures of Homer P. Figg
Zane and the Hurricane

Abduction
(written with Lynn Harnett)

SERIES

DEAR AMERICA: MY NAME IS AMERICA
The Journal of Douglas Allen Deeds,
The Donner Party Expedition, 1846

THE HOUSE ON CHERRY STREET
(written with Lynn Harnett)
The Haunting
The Horror
The Final Nightmare

THE WEREWOLF CHRONICLES
(written with Lynn Harnett)
Night Creature
Children of the Wolf
The Wereing

VISITORS
(written with Lynn Harnett)
Strange Invaders
Things
Brain Stealers

THE
BIG DARK

RODMAN PHILBRICK

THE BLUE SKY PRESS

An Imprint of Scholastic Inc.
New York

With love to Jan Bamberger,
who was there when the story began

Geomagnetic Interference (GMI):

A massive disruption of the Earth's magnetic field that affects electrical circuits. Such a disturbance may interrupt, obstruct, or otherwise degrade or limit the effective performance of the circuit. In an extreme case, electricity as we know it fails.

"Conductive Phenomena Related to Massive Solar Events"
Journal of Applied Physics
Joseph D. Mangano, PhD

1
THE NIGHT THAT CHANGED EVERYTHING

Where were you when the lights went out?

I was in Harmony, New Hampshire, on a night so cold you could sneeze icicles, watching the aurora borealis break-dance across the Milky Way. It was New Year's Eve, of course, we all remember that, those of us who survived. Most of the folks in Harmony (population 857 at the time) were out on a snowy baseball field, in the night shadows of the White Mountains, watching the sky go nuts. Me and my mom and my sister and most of my friends, we all saw it. Our science teacher, Mr. Mangano, had set up his telescope, but really you didn't need a telescope. All you needed to do was open your eyes and look up.

My name is Charlie Cobb. Everybody has their own story about the event or the pulse or whatever you want to call it. Must be, what, seven billion stories? This is mine. What happened when the big dark came to our little town, and what King Man did in the crazy cold, and the long trek down the mountain, all of it.

Like everybody else that night, we thought we knew what to expect. The so-called northern lights would be visible as far south as Cuba, on account of a wicked big sun storm. Something about the solar wind hitting Earth's atmosphere and putting on a light show. Mr. Mangano explained how it was a stream of hot gases belched out by the sun, and something about charged particles, whatever they are. All we really needed to know, me and my friends, was that we had a great excuse to be out late on New Year's Eve. Outside in the dark of night, and not having to watch the stupid ball drop on boring old TV while they droned on about the cute, sad things that happened over the past year.

Except it wasn't dark that night. Me and my best friend, Gronk, we planned to set off some cherry bombs at midnight, but the sky was so bright his mom caught us before we had the chance to take off our mittens. It was so bright there were shadows on the snow, like in the daytime. It was so bright it almost hurt to watch, except you couldn't not watch because you might miss something spectacular.

When I think about it now, looking back, it was, like, super spooky, but at the time we thought it was really cool. People were *ooh*ing and *ahh*ing like at real fireworks. *Oh did you see that one*, and *Wow that was amazing*. And it *was* amazing. There were sheets of shimmering green and shivering purple, and weird little flashes of red along the horizon, and colors no one could quite describe because we'd never seen anything like it. Imagine a lightning bolt hitting a box of crayons and turning it into colored steam. Like that. Electric colors rippling and pulsing as if they were alive. Colors so insane you almost forgot how cold it was, or maybe the cold made it more intense somehow.

Like I said, most of the folks in Harmony were out on the baseball field that night, watching the light show and trying to keep warm. Moms and dads and little kids in puffy snowsuits. Some of the cars and SUVs had been left running so the owners could duck in and get a blast from the heaters. Everybody seemed happy to be there, witnessing something strange and beautiful.

When it got to be ten minutes to midnight, somebody started shouting out a countdown and we all joined in. Ten minutes to the New Year! Nine minutes to the New Year! Like that. We'd gotten to seven minutes or so when it happened. A flash. Okay, more than a flash. Way more. A burst of light that filled the entire sky and whited out the stars, like the universe was trying to take a picture of planet Earth.

I heard Mr. Mangano shout, "Close your eyes!" but it was too late, and for a couple of awful seconds it was like I'd gone blind. But I wasn't blind at all. The lights had gone out. The lights from the sky, the pulsing northern lights, they were gone. And the red taillights and the soft dashboard lights from the cars and SUVs, and the lights from every

3

house and building in Harmony, all suddenly switched off.

It happened so fast that everybody gasped in surprise. And then some little kid started crying, and we could all hear his mother saying not to worry, it was just a blackout, a power failure like happened during the last snowstorm.

"They'll fix it soon," she promised.

Just then someone tugged on my sleeve. My sister, Rebecca. Also known as Becca or sometimes the Beckster. She's not quite a year younger than me, but we're both in the same grade because Becca is wicked smart. I mean scary smart sometimes, like she can figure out what I'm thinking. Or let me know what she's thinking without having to say so.

It was too dark for me to see her face, but I could tell she was worried.

"Charlie," she said in her husky voice. "My flashlight doesn't work. Something is wrong."

Boy was she right about that.

2
BEEP BEEP, THIS WASN'T A TEST

The thing with Becca's mini flashlight, the one she wears on a lanyard cord around her neck? It was a present from my dad when she was little, to make her feel safer when she woke up with night terrors. She hasn't had that kind of nightmare in a long time, but she keeps the flashlight close. Probably it reminds her of Dad and all that.

At the moment, though, her flashlight was the least of our problems. Because as everybody understands now, it wasn't any normal blackout. It wasn't just the electrical grid that had gone down. Cars, trucks, generators, batteries, flashlights, tablets, all the phones, all the planes in the air—everything that used electricity had failed at exactly the same moment.

It was like the entire world had been switched off.

Of course we didn't know that up in Harmony, not right away. It came to us gradual. That night it was the cars and pickup trucks and SUVs. Those that were running quit, and the rest wouldn't start. Turn the key and nothing happened. Every vehicle was dark and getting colder by the moment, and people didn't know what was going on or how to get home. Some could walk home in the starlight, but others lived miles away. And like I said, it was cold enough to sneeze icicles.

My family, we were lucky because our house was only a few blocks from the baseball field. First thing Mom said was "Give me your hands. We have to stick together. Understand?"

All we really understood that night, me and Becca, was that the fun had stopped all of a sudden. One second it was party time under the northern lights, the next it was dark and cold and scary.

Anyhow, Mom knew the way well enough to lead us home. Inside the house it was black as night. Mom told us to wait in the hall and then made her way into the kitchen. We could hear her stumbling a bit and opening and closing drawers. Next thing her worried face was glowing in the light of a candle. "At least this works," she said. "Charlie, I'm putting you in charge of the woodstove. I'm going to place another candle on top of it so you can see, and you will load the stove and start a fire and keep it going."

I could do that, even though my hands were shaking, and not just from the cold that was already starting to creep into the house, which is normally heated by oil, like most of the houses in the north country.

Mom? She went back to the ball field with her candle and gathered up a bunch of the folks who were stranded and brought them to our place, where we all sat around in the glow of the woodstove.

It was really late but nobody wanted to fall asleep. Not without knowing what would happen next.

"It'll come back on," someone said, voice cracking in the dark. "Might take a day or two. Until then we'll get by with generators."

A lot of the folks in Harmony had generators. We did, too—a good one, supposed to come on automatically if the power failed. Except it hadn't come on.

Never did. Wouldn't turn over, wouldn't start.

That's mostly what I remember about the first night, sitting around in the warmth of the woodstove with folks I sort of knew, but who were strangers, really. All of us scared, even the grown-ups, and it was the grown-ups who did most of the talking.

"It was the flash. It did something. Knocked the power out."

"Huh! That science teacher guy said something about a solar flare. That's why the sky was so crazy. I lived here all my life, I never seen northern lights like that."

Someone else spoke up. "Power goes out, no big deal, right? Happens now and then. Usually when a storm puts trees down on the wires, or maybe a transformer blows. But this is different. Batteries all dead? Car batteries, phone batteries? Every kind of battery not functioning? It ain't right."

"No, sir, it ain't right. You know those annoying emergency alerts they do on TV and radio? Beep beep, this is a test? If this was a real emergency, you'd have been instructed to tune to a local station? Has anybody tried that, tuning to a local station?"

Mom explained that we had an Emergency Alert System radio in the kitchen, but it wasn't working. "I went through all the double As in my spare drawer. Either the batteries are dead or the radio is, or both."

Somebody cursed, I'm not sure who.

Mom said, kind but firm, "Not in front of the children, please. You want to curse the situation, be my guest, but do it outside. So. Anybody want hot chocolate? I can heat some up on the woodstove. Can't make the radio work, or fix your cars, or explain what happened, but I can make hot chocolate."

"Thank you, Mrs. Cobb. We're a little stressed is all."

"Understood. And please call me Emma."

"Thank you, Emma. For coming out with that candle and finding us in the cold of night. Thank you for inviting us into your home. And thank you for the hot chocolate."

"But I haven't made it yet!"

"Thank you just the same."

Took forever for the sun to rise, and for a time I worried maybe it wouldn't. Like maybe the sun had blinked out or blown itself up. But it came up normal enough, edging over the horizon, a hot blob too bright to look at directly, and soon we could feel the heat of it coming through the windows. So planet Earth was still turning, and the sun was still burning.

Only thing missing was electricity.

3
THE FIRST DAY AFTER

That sun made us all feel better. By ten o'clock it was warm enough to melt the top layer of snow, and folks were saying the power would be restored soon. Maybe not in the north country, but for sure down in Manchester and Nashua. Then the TV news would come back on and explain what had happened and how long it would take to fix.

Like we were making up for being so scared that first night by acting hopeful today.

"You know what? With the sun on the hood and the battery warmed, I bet that car will start," said one of our overnight guests, and everybody pretty much agreed.

Except everybody was wrong. Mom cleaned the terminals on our Ford Explorer and tightened down the battery connections, but it didn't make any difference. It was dead. Same with our so-called automatic generator. Everything that depended on electricity was stone dead.

Mom finally gave up fiddling with the generator. Nothing doing. "When Joe said the solar flare might disrupt power, he wasn't kidding, was he?"

Joe is Mr. Mangano, our science teacher. Mom teaches at the same school, the younger grades. Mr. Mangano has the middle-school kids, and that includes me and Becca.

"This thing with all the batteries being dead, that's worrisome," Mom said. "Charlie, you're still in charge of keeping the house warm. That means feeding the stove, stacking the wood, moving an adequate supply into the house. Don't want to let those pipes freeze."

"Sure, Mom. No problem." Normally we might have left a faucet dripping at night, so the pipes wouldn't freeze, but no power meant no water pressure because the well pump wasn't working.

Amazing what depends on electricity.

"Becca, you will gather up buckets of snow and melt them near the stove. Then pour the melt water into the downstairs tub. We'll need it for washing and cooking. For drinking we have enough bottled water for a few days at least. After that we'll need to bring the melt water to a boil."

"After that?" said Becca, her eyes big.

"This could go on for a little while, honey. We have to be prepared. Plan for the worst and hope for the best."

"I *hate* this!"

"Nobody likes it. But from this moment on, we will do our best not to complain, understood? And thank our lucky stars we don't live way out in the woods or farther up the mountain. We can walk to the Superette and the school and visit our neighbors. So it could be worse."

"That's what you always say."

Mom laughed. "Because it's always true. Chin up, Becca."

Chin up. My dad used to say that. The Beckster was worried sick—she's always been the family worrier—but she fetched buckets of snow like Mom asked, and after a while she got into it, estimating how many gallons were stored in the tub.

"Five gallons! Know how much snow had to melt to make five measly gallons? Forty pails!"

I'd pretty much caught up with the woodstove—the house was practically toasty—when Gronk pounded on our front door.

"Sorry, the bell don't ring."

"Doesn't!" Mom called from the kitchen.

"Yes, Mrs. Cobb."

Gronk's real name is Gary Small. He used to make snorting dinosaur noises, *gronk-gronk-gronk*, when he was little, and the name stuck.

Mom came out of the kitchen. "Are you hungry, Gary? How's everything at your house?"

"I'm always hungry. We're okay. My dad sent me over to tell you there's a meeting at the school."

*　　*　　*

The meeting was held on the steps outside the school, because with the sun shining it was actually warmer outside than inside the building. No school that day because it was a holiday, remember, but Harmony Center School is right in the center of Harmony (big surprise) so it made sense to gather there and share information.

Not that anyone had information. Not the selectmen, not the school principal, nobody. Nobody knew nuthin'.

Which didn't stop them talking about it.

"There was a flash and everything went dead, am I right? We all saw it."

"Yeah, okay, a solar flare knocks out the grid, we heard that could happen. But this? This is crazy."

"You know what's crazy? I yanked on my snowblower for an hour. Nothing. And that sucker always starts on the first pull."

"Flooded her, maybe?"

"Trouble is there's no spark. Same with my truck. No spark!"

"Don't make sense!"

The only one with any new information was Mr. Mangano, who arrived last, cupping something small in his hands. Everybody shut up because before he became a teacher, Joseph Mangano used to be an actual scientist, launching weather balloons and measuring the atmosphere and cool stuff like that.

"Anybody else checked a compass? No? Strange thing. Not sure what it means, but there's a faint chance it might lead to an explanation of the phenomena."

"Phenomena? What are you talking about, Joe?"

"The electrical phenomena, or rather the lack of electrical conduction. See? The compass no longer points to magnetic north. It isn't pointed anywhere. It wanders. And all the magnets on my refrigerator dropped off. Can't find a magnet that still works."

"So? What's that got to do with my truck won't start?"

Mr. Mangano sounded almost apologetic. "Just a theory, but whatever happened last night, maybe it kicked off a geomagnetic event."

"Pretend we're kids in your class, Joe."

"Sure, of course." He cleared his throat. "Earth generates a magnetic field. That's part of what keeps the good stuff inside our atmosphere and the bad stuff out. That's why the compass points to the magnetic north pole. But we know that the magnetic poles have shifted, or even switched completely, north for south, many times in the past. Last time was 780,000 years ago, which means we're about 250,000 years overdue, going by averages. We don't know what exactly happens during a geomagnetic event, or how long it takes. Last time around there wasn't any power grid, or cars or batteries or cell phones. Or humans, for that matter."

"You're getting all this 'cause a Boy Scout compass don't work?"

"Just a theory. I'm probably wrong."

"That's nuts is what that is."

Mr. Mangano was about to reply when the first gunshot echoed like a crack of thunder in the mountains.

4
HEAR THE WHISTLE BLOW

Have you ever seen a postcard of a small New England town? That's pretty much how Harmony looked the day after the lights went out. The postcard version usually has a church with a white steeple and a small park with a monument to dead soldiers and a block or two of simple wooden buildings for the general store and a bank and a police station. Except we didn't have a bank, exactly, just a glorified ATM, and no police station because there was only one cop, and he was a part-time volunteer, and instead of a general store we had the Superette.

The gunshot came from the vicinity of the ATM. In the confusion, me and Gronk slipped away from the school steps, crossed the block, and sneaked near enough to see what was happening.

A bunch of folks had been waiting in line to take money out, and some of them had their hands in the air, like they were ready to surrender. The

16

ATM had a glass cubicle to protect it from the weather. One of the glass walls had been shattered, but it looked like nobody got hurt. Turned out the ATM wasn't working—big surprise with the power out, duh—but they were waiting in line anyway, in case it came back on.

The guy with the gun wasn't pointing it at them, exactly, but he was waving it around, which explained the hands in the air.

"Stand back!" he yelled. "I'll get 'er open!"

Me and Gronk hid behind a stalled pickup truck. Better safe than sorry. "Looks like an AR-15," Gronk said, peeking over the side of the truck.

The man with the assault rifle was dressed in winter hunting camo and knee-high black boots, and had a lumpy backpack slung over one shoulder. His back was turned to me, but he looked familiar. Even the gun looked familiar.

"That's Mr. Bragg," Gronk hissed. "My dad always said he was a nut bar."

"The dude with the weird eyes?"

"Yup."

Mom had told us to stay away from Webster Bragg. He and his family, including five adult sons and their wives and children, had moved to Harmony a few years ago. They converted an old farmhouse into a compound and surrounded the whole place with barbed wire to "keep the feds out." According to the billboards they erected on the property, the Braggs were opposed to any form of government and any kind of tax, and any race other than the white race. The one thing they did favor was guns. The women never left the compound, but Bragg and his sons made a point of walking around the village with rifles slung over their shoulders, because New Hampshire is an open-carry state. Once in a while they passed out pamphlets about conspiracies and stuff, but mostly they kept to themselves. Like I said, the female members of the family stayed in the compound, out of sight, and when Bragg went out he did all the talking. His boys kept their mouths shut and followed his orders.

It was kind of scary at first, dudes with assault rifles, but they never threatened anyone, and after a while you hardly noticed.

Until the rifles started firing.

"What's he doing?" I asked Gronk.

"Get down!"

We covered our heads and dropped to the snowy road as Mr. Bragg opened fire on the ATM. Must have gone through the whole clip, but it didn't do any good, that ATM refused to cough up any cash. Which really made him mad.

"See?" he shouted. "This is what I'm talking about! Think this is an accident, everything failing at the same time? It's no accident! They've been planning this for years!"

Bragg was a tall, rugged dude with a bristly beard and eyes so pale they looked almost white. He had a bare-shaven upper lip that was usually curled in disdain, so that he looked like a mean version of Abraham Lincoln.

"Web, would you please put down the gun?" one of the men in line asked. "You're scaring people."

"They should be scared! Not of me or this firearm! No, sir! They should be scared of those who did this to us!"

"You know something we don't?"

Hearing the question, Bragg seemed to puff up, and his strange pale eyes flashed. "Maybe I do! Look around! Don't be fooled! That big show in the sky last night? Ha! That was a distraction! Cutting off the power and the phones and the TV and the money, that's only the beginning! The first salvo! This is a war, just like me and my boys have been predicting! Good against evil! Dark against light!"

He went on like that for a while, and eventually most of the folks who had been in line backed away and left him to it. Some headed across the street to the Superette, where another long line had formed, but a few people hung back, wanting to hear what Mr. Webster Bragg had to say about the mysterious failure of electricity, and how it was caused by a worldwide Jewish conspiracy in league with dark-skinned mongrel people, and maybe the United Nations, too.

Mom had always said Webster Bragg was a hatemonger. I was never quite sure what that meant, until he started spewing that ugly stuff at the ATM.

Now I knew.

I dusted the snow off my pants. "I better get home."

"Yeah. Me, too," said Gronk.

We didn't get more than a block before the shouting resumed, this time outside the Superette. And this time Mr. Bragg was backed up by three of his big, burly sons, who were wearing identical camo. None of them had eyes quite like their dad's, and as usual they let him do all the talking. But they looked dangerous for sure, with holstered handguns and assault rifles slung over their shoulders, ready to react if their father gave the command.

"You think this is a coincidence?" Mr. Bragg roared, his big voice booming. "ATMs quit? Debit cards don't work? Cash sales only? They knew! They were ready! All part of the plan!"

"Who knew?"

"Her! The Jew manager! She's in on it! Wake up, people! Wake up, or they'll take your freedom from you while you sleep!"

Mr. Bragg had his AR-15 slung over his shoulder, not aiming at anyone, but the way he was ranting on about conspiracies and secret government spies was almost as scary as when the bullets were flying. Like he was trying to get people on his side before he did something bad to the Superette manager, Mrs. Adler.

"You think you know her, but you don't! That's how they infiltrate. They live among us, gaining our trust. They lull us into complacency. And then they strike when we least expect it!"

"Who's 'they'? What are you saying? Did you hear something?"

Bragg studied the crowd and shook his head in disbelief, like he wasn't sure we were ready to hear the truth. "All I'm saying, the witch who runs this place won't take my sovereign gold, and that's a sure sign of where her true loyalties lie."

"Gold?"

"Paper money is just paper, okay? I mean think about it. Trade a piece of dirty paper for a can of beans? Give workers pieces of paper in exchange for their labor? It makes no sense, but we've been brainwashed into thinking paper is worth something. Diluting our economy with paper money is how it all started."

When grown-ups talk about money my ears kind of go on vacation, so I won't pretend I understood what Mr. Bragg was saying about a New World Order trying to enslave us with paper dollars, and secret United Nations troops preparing to invade, and black helicopters, and so on. But some of those in line at the Superette started nodding along like he was making sense, and when Bragg raised his AR-15 and announced that he intended to liberate the supermarket, nobody tried to stop him.

"This is how it starts!" he shouted, firing a shot in the air. "This is how we take back our freedom!"

He and his sons were about to invade the Superette when suddenly a whistle blew. Everybody seemed to freeze.

"Hold it right there!"

Standing on the snowy street, hands cocked on his hips, was a man with a referee's whistle looped around his neck.

Reggie Kingman, the school custodian.

5
THOSE WHO NEED

To be honest, I never paid much attention to Mr. Kingman until that whistle blew. As I said, he was the custodian at Harmony Center School, but that was his day job. Had been since he came back home after his young wife died, many years ago. On the side he was the volunteer police officer, which mostly meant he put on a uniform and saluted the flag when we had school assemblies or parades.

He wasn't like a real policeman because there's not much crime in Harmony. If something serious happened, like the time Boonie Givens got drunk and pretended to take his wife and children hostage, the state police came over from Twin Mountain and took care of it. At school some of the kids called him Barf Man behind his back, because he was the poor dude who mopped up the mess when somebody hurled. As the volunteer police officer, Mr.

Kingman got taken more serious, but not by everybody. I heard one of the teachers remark that Reggie was our own Barney Fife. In case you don't know, that's a character from an old TV show, and it wasn't meant as a compliment. Maybe because he took the cop job so seriously, with his buttons and belt and boots all polished, and the way he snapped to attention when the flag passed.

Barf Man. Barney Fife. It all changed that day at the Superette.

"What seems to be the problem?" he said, standing ramrod straight, chin out and hat high.

"None of your beeswax!" barked Mr. Bragg. "We'll handle this our way!"

Kingman shook his head. "Stand down, Mr. Bragg. Lower your weapon. That's an order."

A couple of the people in the crowd actually laughed, but in an uneasy kind of way, as if they weren't sure what was going on, or if they should really be part of it.

Bragg brandished the AR-15. "I'm the one with the weapon! I'll be giving the orders around here!"

Officer Kingman had a pistol on his black leather belt, part of his uniform, but he didn't unclip the holster. His hands stayed right where they were, with his thumbs hooked into his belt. Without raising his voice or sounding excited, he said, "This is New Hampshire. Everybody has a gun. Lower the weapon, Mr. Bragg, and ask your boys to do the same."

Bragg hesitated, looked around at the crowd, and finally lowered the AR-15. His sons stood at ease, hands off their guns, but Bragg remained at the head of his little family army, not backing down.

"What you gonna do, Mr. Janitor?" he sneered. "What's your plan?"

Officer Kingman ignored that. He spotted one of the Superette employees and asked for the store manager. Took a minute, but Mrs. Adler emerged with a frightened look on her face. Stood there kind of stiff and defensive with *Shop Smart at the Superette!* on her store apron.

"I understand there's been a dispute about the price of groceries."

She shook her head vigorously. "We haven't jacked up the prices, if that's what you're implying. But with the registers and card readers down, it has to be cash. What else can I do?"

"How are supplies?"

Mrs. Adler looked a little more confident—this was her area of expertise. She'd been running the Superette for as long as I could remember. "We stocked up before the holiday, so inventory is strong. The pharmacy is well stocked. Freezers are packed and will stay cold for the time being. But another day like this will wipe us out. People are hoarding, that's what it is."

"Hoarding?"

"This guy?" She jerked her thumb at Mr. Bragg. "Tried to swap a couple of itsy little coins for every can of tuna on the shelf, plus all the peanut butter."

"Gold sovereigns, lady, worth hundreds of dollars! It was a good deal!"

"Maybe so. But if I give it all to you, what about those who haven't been able to get to the store yet, or don't have provisions laid by for an emergency?" She turned to Kingman. "We had to start rationing, officer. Ten cans to the customer, that's the new rule."

"And those who don't have cash?" Kingman asked.

She hesitated, avoiding eye contact with Mr. Bragg. "We've been writing down names and the amount. Customers will settle up once the power comes back on."

"Sounds like you got it under control, Mrs. Adler. And you're right to be worried about those without provisions. We have some elderly who don't have much in the cupboard."

Webster Bragg, hearing that, started to edge away, the AR-15 slung over his back. His sons followed.

"We could use your help, Mr. Bragg," Kingman called out. "Rumor has it you and your family have lots of food stockpiled at your compound. Freeze-dried, canned, all kinds. Enough to survive for years. Any truth to those rumors?"

"None of your beeswax! What's mine is mine!"

"No argument here." Kingman turned back to the crowd. "How about those of you in line? Anybody know anyone who might need assistance? Folks who can't get to the store or haven't got a wood-stove for backup? The temperature is a concern, as cold as it's been. And drinking water could be a problem."

Later I decided it wasn't the whistle that did it, put Reggie Kingman in charge. It was him asking who needed help.

6
MIGHT, MIGHT, MIGHT

The thing about my mom, when she got mad she got real quiet, which was way scarier than yelling.

"I'm sorry, okay? We didn't know what was going on," I tried to explain as the three of us walked home, snow squeaking under our boots.

"Exactly my point."

"He was only shooting the ATM, not people."

"'Only' the ATM? That's lame, Charlie. You're better than that."

"It was stupid, I know."

We kept trudging along while Mom thought it over. Becca didn't say a word. I wouldn't, either, if it was her about to get punished. With Mom, excuses only made it worse.

Mom took a deep breath, exhaling steam. "Under normal circumstances you'd be grounded. Phone privilege suspended. No devices, no TV. Obviously that's pointless, given the situation. So

all I can do is ask you to think before you put yourself in danger, and remember that family comes
first."

"Of course, Mom. Absolutely."

She placed her mittens on my shoulders and
gave me a squeeze. "Nobody knows what's going
on, or what really happened, and that makes things
dangerous. I mean, come on, the power has been
out for less than twenty-four hours, and already
there are men waving guns and spouting non-
sense? You keep away from all that, and especially
from Webster Bragg. Stick close to home, clear?"

"Clear."

We were coming up the walkway to the house.
The wind had picked up, and snow was sifting
into the shoveled path.

"Becca, honey, you're good with arithmetic, so I
need your help taking an inventory of food, medicine, and supplies on hand. Charlie, you're in
charge of heat. See if you can get a sense of how
many days before we run out of wood."

"We've got three cords, Mom. That's enough
for the whole winter."

She looked at me, eyes smiling. "You're absolutely sure? Please think it through, sweet pea.
Study, think, solve. That's all I ask."

Sometimes it stinks to have a mom who's a
schoolteacher because everything is like a lesson.
Study the problem, think about the problem, solve
the problem. Blah blah blah. But as usual, she was
right because once I really thought about it and
made a few calculations, it was pretty obvious that

if our stack of firewood was the only source of heat, it couldn't possibly last through the whole winter.

That's what Mom was saying without saying it. Our woodstove wasn't just a stove, it was a hungry mouth that needed to be fed, and its food—our woodpile—wouldn't last forever. Kept going like this, twenty-four hours a day, the pile might last four or five weeks. Maybe. Longer if we got a thaw. Less if it got even colder.

But hey, what was I worried about? It wasn't like electricity was gone forever. This would be over long before the firewood ran out. Bound to be. Had to be. Right?

Right?

The next few days seemed to be mostly about waiting. Waiting for the power to come back on, and the lights and the phones and the TV, and everything else electric. Only it wasn't like waiting for Christmas or your birthday, which can be fun. More like waiting for your parachute to open before you hit the ground.

Mom got everything organized, of course, and Becca was into it, too, following Mom around with her notepad and her pencil with the big eraser that looked like a pink clown nose. Taking inventory and figuring out weekly menus, because Mom needed to keep her blood sugar balanced, and we all needed certain nutrients, and boring stuff like that.

Officer Kingman came by on the second day, conducting what he called a "welfare check."

"Hello, Emma. We're knocking on doors in the village," he explained, holding his hat in his hands. "Evaluating the well-being of every resident, how they're fixed for wood and food and water and so on."

"Big job."

"Yeah it is, but I'm not alone. First thing I did was deputize volunteers to check on the more remote homes. Some of those places are accessible only by snowmobile or snowshoe this time of year, and snowmobiles are out."

Mom invited him into the foyer. "The Carters keep horses," she suggested. "That might help."

"We did consider that. But it turns out the snow is too deep for horses. You'd have to dig a path for them first. Faster on snowshoes."

Mom nodded. "Everything okay out there?"

"Not even close, but we're making do."

"My sister, Beth, is in the New Hampshire Air National Guard, on active duty. I keep expecting her to show up on our doorstep, let us know what's going on in the rest of the world."

"Oh yeah? Where's she stationed?"

"Portsmouth."

He looked disappointed. "Way downstate, then. Must be a hundred miles from here." He added, "I haven't seen a plane in the sky. Have you?"

Mom shook her head. Suddenly she seemed worried sick.

His face fell. "I'm sure Beth is fine, Emma, but I'll bet they're keeping her pretty busy, planes or no planes. Emergency like this they'd mobilize everyone in uniform."

"I'm sure you're right."

"All we can do, given the situation, is tend to our own. So I'll mark you down as healthy, warm, and well-provisioned, shall I?"

"We'll be fine. And Reggie? That thing at the Superette, with that bully and his sons? Well done."

He put on his hat, ready to be on his way. "Thanks, Emma. It worked out. Next time it might not be so easy. Be nice if the lights come on soon. Until then, keep warm, stay hydrated."

I'm ashamed to say that's the first time I gave a thought to Aunt Beth's situation. Who, for all my mother knew, might have been in the air when the pulse hit. Might have crashed, might be dead or injured.

Might, might, might.

I was really sick of might.

7
WHAT SHE SMELLED

The next bad thing happened three days later, after we'd settled into our boring routine of keeping the house from freezing and ourselves from starving. And not just us—Mom started preparing food for some of the old geezers who couldn't remain in their homes without heat. Reggie Kingman had arranged for them to stay at Moulton House. There's no longer any Moulton family in Harmony, but after croaking or retiring or whatever, their original house got turned into a museum. Or that's the story they tell when you take the tour. Anyhow, the Moulton place, a rickety old colonial, had a fireplace in every room. Insulation wasn't so good, but with the fires blazing it kept the chill off, and was close enough to the center of town so folks could lend a hand, bringing in water and food and so on.

Where Kingman got the wood to keep those fireplaces going I don't know. Firewood had suddenly become more precious than food. A lot of the families had freezers full of venison, so no one was going hungry, but not many had enough wood to feel really safe if it meant getting through a long, hard winter. Everybody with an ax was out chopping down trees—me included—but the wood was green and frozen solid and hard to cut up with a handsaw. Probably used up more calories chopping and sawing than you got burning.

Burning. Fire. You see where this is going. What happens when fire trucks don't work, and pumpers can't pump, and the only way to fight a fire is with your bare hands and a bucket of snow.

First we heard of it was Gronk pounding on the door and bellowing, "Superette's on fire!"

By the time we got there it was too late. Not that we could have done much. Nobody could. The fire consuming the Superette was so hot and bright it hurt to look. Inside the boiling inferno, rows of shelves twisted and curled as if alive, making screaming metal noises. The heat intensified, driving us back. Then a massive pair of flames whooshed up through the roof and joined like clasping hands. A moment later the building caved in on itself, roaring as if in pain.

Poor Mrs. Adler, the manager, wandered around in her orange parka, tears streaming down her chubby red face. Not saying much of anything, just staring at the flames and shaking her head.

When I came up behind her to say I was sorry about the Superette, she nearly jumped out of her skin.

"Sorry, Mrs. Adler."

"It's only a building," she said, her eyes searching the dark. "I got away, that's what counts, right?"

"Sure, Mrs. Adler."

She started to say something else, changed her mind, and then Kingman blew his famous whistle to get the crowd's attention. "Listen up! See all those sparks? We have to suppress the sparks or the fire will spread. Boots and buckets, folks! Boots and buckets!"

And sure enough, burning sparks floated through the winter night like little parachutes on fire. They kept smoldering even after they settled on the frozen ground. Some we could stamp out, but others had to be smothered under a bucket of snow. Must have been fifty of us running around and stamping out the sparks. Everything seemed strangely dim because the night sky was overcast—no moon or stars—and the only light was from the smoldering wreckage of the Superette. We kept bumping into one another as we ran to stomp the sparks. Kind of funny, really, and Gronk and me got to giggling as we pretended to be Godzilla staggering around in the dark, *stomp stomp*.

Finally the sparks settled down, and we all stopped running around and warmed our hands at the glowing wreck of our only grocery store and pharmacy. Nobody said much, not even Reggie

Kingman, who looked taller in the glow of the fire. When the fire was contained and things seemed pretty safe, he came around shaking mittens and thanking us.

"I think we can handle it from here," he said. "You folks go on home and get some sleep. Things will improve tomorrow."

It was a nice thing to say, but I'm pretty sure he didn't really believe it. I was just a kid, but I understood that things would only improve when the power returned, and motors started, and cell phones worked. But in a weird, sick way it had almost been fun, fighting the fire together. Until your brain bumped up against the fact that this wasn't a bonfire intended for our entertainment, it was the Superette, and now it was gone, maybe forever.

When Kingman got to Mrs. Adler he gave her a big hug, and then in the middle of the hug he seemed to freeze.

"What?" he said, stepping back and trying to see her expression in the faint glow of the smoldering ashes. "What did you say?"

Mrs. Adler looked stricken, no surprise, but she also looked frightened. Not scared of the fire so much as just afraid. "They were after me, I think. I was lucky to get away."

"Who was after you?"

"Whoever set the fire. It was the smell that saved me. Kerosene. I came out of my office to check on that smell, and then the hallway burst into flame. It was smoky but I caught a glimpse of him running away, on the other side of the flames."

"Who, Naomi?" Kingman asked. "Who did this?"

"He was running away, you know? All I could tell was that he was young. And he was wearing camouflage."

By then most of those who had come out to help were gathered around, and as soon as they heard *camouflage*, someone in the crowd shouted, "Bragg! You saying Webster Bragg did this?"

"Not him," Mrs. Adler said, shaking her head. "Younger."

"One of his sons! Had to be! They didn't get what they wanted so they burned down our only store, our only pharmacy! So what are we gonna do about it?"

The idea caught fire almost as quick as the Superette. Several things seemed to happen at the same time. Angry talk about marching out to Bragg's compound, maybe setting it on fire to teach him a lesson. My mother grabbed the back of my jacket and yanked me away from the crowd. And Reggie Kingman gave a toot on his whistle.

"Whoa! Hold it right there! We need to calm down and think about this."

"Think about what? We know it was him, and you know it, too."

Kingman had both hands up like he was slowing traffic. "That may be, but we're not going to do to him what he might have done to Mrs. Adler, based on suspicion. I'm calling a town meeting for tomorrow. We'll meet in the light of day and we'll decide together, as a town, not as a mob."

There were some mumbled protests, but that pretty much did it. The crowd broke up and we headed home.

On the way Becca asked Mom why anyone would do such a terrible thing.

"I wish I knew, chipmunk." She linked her arms through ours. "I wish I knew."

I had a question, too. One I didn't dare ask.

Who was next?

8
GRONK HAS AN ANSWER

Kingman called a town meeting for the next afternoon, to discuss the fire, but the weather got in the
way. The sky stayed hard and gray all morning,
and then at noon the snow began to fall. The first
few inches were fluffy, covering the remains of the
Superette like a soft white blanket, and then something tightened in the frozen air and a blizzard was
suddenly upon us.

Stick your head outside and BB-sized pellets of
snow would scratch your face with icy fingernails
and snatch your breath away.

Not that it made us forget what happened to the
Superette. Everybody seemed to think it was Mr.
Bragg, seeking revenge. Or one of his sons following orders. Had to be. But before the town could
figure out what to do about it, we had to survive
the worst blizzard in years.

If the power hadn't already been out, the storm would have killed it for sure. The snow turned heavy, snapping branches and clotting up the windows, making it dark long before sundown. Not that we ever saw the sun that day. All we could see was the white of the storm punching us in the face, and the mad moaning of the wind, and the knuckle-crack of birch trees snapping, killed by the weight of the snow.

Couldn't get outside to fetch firewood, no way. Luckily Becca and I had stacked wood all around the house, including the basement, and we fed that stove like it was a baby bird screaming for worms. The dry heat made our eyeballs ache, but we didn't care. Keeping out the cold, that's all we cared about. The wind sucked at the chimney like it was a straw, making the woodstove glow, and Mom said it was a banshee of a blizzard, the way it screamed and moaned.

"A banshee is an Irish ghost," she explained. "I don't believe in ghosts but I do wish the wind would stop. Only thing good about this storm, it's hitting Webster Bragg as hard as it's hitting us. Good luck setting a house afire in weather like this!"

"Poor Mrs. Adler," Becca said, her voice getting very small.

Mom acted like she regretted bringing up the subject. "Mrs. Adler will be fine. We'll all be fine. One day at a time, pumpkin. Hey. Hey. Nobody cries today, and that's an order! Charlie? Find one of those old board games and keep busy, both of you."

Typical of Mom. Keep busy. No matter how rotten or sad you felt, busy would make you better. Anyhow, Becca sniffed back her tears and then beat the crumbs out of me in Scrabble. I bet she knows twice as many words as I do.

"Muzjiks? Really? What does it mean?"

Becca shrugged. "Something Russian, I think. Whatever, it's allowed. You can look it up."

"No I can't," I pointed out. "You're supposed to know what it means."

"It's allowed," she insisted.

The storm rattled the window glass, and the whole house seemed to moan in response.

Becca sighed. "It feels like the end, Charlie. First a fire, then ice. Like the poem."

"What poem?"

"Robert Frost. We're doing a class project on him, remember? Or we were. He wrote a famous poem about how the world ends in fire or ice. What if it's both?"

"The world isn't ending, Becca. It's only a storm, a really bad storm."

Becca pointed to the little flashlight on the cord around her neck. "What about this?"

"Um. Hey. People lived without electricity for a zillion years, right?"

"Yeah, but *we* didn't. We can't even put out a fire."

I wished lots of things. I wished my dad had never gone skiing that day two years ago. I wished the big dark had never happened. I wished Mr.

Bragg would go away and leave us alone. I wished the banshee blizzard would stop.

But mostly I wished I had an answer that would make my sister feel better.

At least one of my wishes came true, because by the time the sun came up the next day, the storm was over. The air was bitter cold, but the wind was gone. And the snow it left behind? That was the bad news, because the snow was now four feet deeper, for a total of about six feet, and the top layer was six inches of ice. So if you had firewood stored outside without cover, it might as well have been buried underground. All those birch trees that came down? Gone, smothered, covered up. As if the whole world had been smoothed out.

It was late in the morning before the message finally got out, carried on foot—snowshoe, mostly—from door to door. Bean supper that afternoon at the town hall, everybody invited. Listen for the bell in the church tower. And, oh yeah, the hall would be heated, so come share the warmth with your neighbors.

Heated? The town hall had an oil burner, and oil burners need electricity, so how was it going to be heated?

Gronk had an answer for that. A joke, I hoped. "Need heat? Invite an arsonist."

Turns out they invited themselves.

9
PLEDGING ALLEGIANCE

It was amazing how many people crawled out of their snowbound homes and made it to the old town hall that afternoon. Trudging through snowdrifts, fighting the tree-snapping cold as the bell rang in the church tower. Bundled up in parkas and snow-mobile suits, faces covered with scarves and ski masks. Some, like us, didn't have far to go. Others had to cover miles of that frozen landscape, but cover it they did, some of them pulling little kids and older folks on plastic sleds and snow tubes. Anything to get there.

At first Mom didn't think we should all go, that we didn't dare leave the woodstove untended, but then she changed her mind. "This could be important. Tamp it down, Charlie. The heat in the house should hold until we get back."

So we tamped down the stove and joined the strange parade. Everybody muffled up like snow zombies, waving their mittens and gloves but not stopping to chat because the air was cold enough to freeze teeth.

Inside the hall it was, as promised, warm and welcoming. Reggie Kingman had brought in a big pellet stove from his own basement. He'd had lots of help, because that stove was so heavy, and they'd run a stovepipe through a window, and stacked bags of wood pellets ready to feed the stove. Gronk and his parents had come early, lending a hand. Tables had been set up, and folding chairs, and stacks of paper bowls and plates and utensils. Like a big indoor picnic. Five or six huge pots of beans and venison chili bubbled on candle-powered warming trays and somehow there were fresh-baked rolls—oh did those smell good—and gallons of fresh-perked coffee and hot chocolate.

Kingman was at the entrance, all duded up in his best uniform, and way more talkative than when he was our school custodian. "Take off your hats and coats and stay awhile," he said, gesturing to the crowd inside. "Have something to eat. Relax. Don't thank me, thank your neighbors. They prepared all this." When asked what he intended to do about the Superette, he said, "We'll take that up after the meal, don't you worry. First things first."

And so we ate. Something about it, the whole town sharing food in the same room, made life feel almost normal. Like even if the power never came back on we would still be able to feed and warm ourselves, and gather as citizens to celebrate the fact that we were all okay.

When everybody was full to groaning, Kingman climbed onto the stage and asked us all to rise and recite the Pledge of Allegiance, like he always did at the school assemblies.

"I pledge allegiance to the flag of the United States of America . . ."

That's as far as we got before Webster Bragg and his sons burst into the town hall, armed to the teeth and looking for trouble.

Warm as it was, everybody froze.

Mr. Bragg grinned, pleased with the impression he'd made, his weird pale eyes gleaming with pleasure. It was so quiet he hardly had to raise his voice to be heard. "Think what you're doing, people! Get it through your heads! America as you knew it no longer exists. This man wants you to pledge allegiance to *him*, that's what this is all about."

Officer Kingman remained at attention, hand on his heart.

"Look at him," Bragg said, shaking his head in disgust. "Barely fit to wash floors, but he thinks he's a cop just because he has a uniform. If he spent as much time thinking as he does polishing his shoes, maybe he'd have a clue. But he doesn't, and that's the problem."

From the back of the hall came a thin, shaky voice. "What about the fire, mister? Mrs. Adler said it was arson. Was it you?"

It was an old man I didn't know. Skinny and frail, his body shaking like his voice, not from fear but from one of those illnesses old people get.

Doubt he weighed as much as a bowl of wet corn-flakes, but there he was, asking the question we all had in our minds.

If Mr. Bragg was troubled by the question he didn't show it. "The fire? Glad you asked. That's the reason we came by this afternoon, to make clear it had nothing to do with me or mine. No way! Anybody who says different is lying. For all I know that Jew manager burned it down herself, to lay the blame on me."

The old man stared at Bragg with watery eyes. "Mrs. Adler said the arsonist was wearing camo. Like you and your sons."

Mr. Bragg snorted and then grinned. "Half the kids in Harmony wear camo-pattern pajamas. Might be one of them, for all I know."

Meanwhile, his boys had fanned out. Scrawnier and younger versions of their father, with similar Lincoln-style beards. Not raising their weapons but casually blocking the exits.

Mom put her hands on our shoulders and whispered, "If I shove you under the table, you go there and stay there. Understood?"

Kind of like a lockdown drill at school. "Shelter in place," they call it. But Mom didn't shove us under the table right away. Maybe because she didn't want to call attention to us—nobody else in the crowd was moving—or maybe because she wasn't sure that hiding under the table would do us much good if the bullets started flying. Maybe we'd be better off making a run for it, find a way through the doors or out a window.

But it never came to that. Nobody opened fire that afternoon at the bean supper. Strangely enough, they barely raised their voices. It was like Webster Bragg and Reggie Kingman were in a contest to see who could be the most calm and reasonable sounding.

Up on the stage, still facing the flag with his hand to his heart, Officer Kingman cleared his throat and continued where he'd left off. "And to the Republic for which it stands, one Nation under God, indivisible, with liberty and justice for all."

After a moment of silence, Bragg began to laugh, *heh-heh-heh*, like a muffled machine gun. "Seriously, Reggie? That's the best you got? That's what you're offering for leadership? A pledge to a piece of faded cloth, to a nation that no longer exists?"

"How do you know the nation no longer exists?" Kingman asked. "Based on what?"

Bragg tapped his own forehead. "Based on this. On my ability to think and reason. On my ability to see the big picture. When I say the nation no longer exists, I don't mean the population, I mean the federal government. Democracy is dead, flicked off like a switch. And I say good riddance! It was weak and deserved to die, and that's the truth. We have to face the facts, folks. The enemies of reason won the first battle. They destroyed the power grid and pulled the plug on civilization and nothing will ever be the same again."

Reggie nodded along, as if considering the merits of the argument. "What about our science teacher's theory? That whatever happened, it was kicked off by a solar flare, a big one?"

Again the machine-gun laugh, *heh-heh-heh*. Bragg shook his head like he felt sorry for anybody who believed such a foolish thing. "You want to blame it on the sun, you go ahead. I know the flash of a nuclear warhead when I see one! Timed it for when we'd all be looking up, for maximum effect. They been planning this for years, waiting for the right moment."

"They?" Kingman asked. "Who is 'they'?"

"The forces of darkness," Bragg said ominously, his strange pale eyes gone cold. "The mongrel races that thrive on chaos."

"Who is that exactly?"

Bragg looked faintly disgusted by the stupidity of the question. "Some call it the New World Order, but that's just a name. Whatever we call them, they are those who conspire to rule the world. Those that have risen from the mud. Mixed-race, mongrel breeds. Blacks and Jews. And they're coming, mark my word. We have to be ready to defend ourselves. And we won't have a chance if we refuse to see what's right before our eyes."

"And what's that, Mr. Bragg?" Kingman asked.

"A fool in a phony uniform. A fool who thinks he's a hero when we all know he's barely fit to swab the filth out of our toilets. You, Reggie Kingman, you're the fool, and so is anyone fool enough to believe you could lead them."

10
CONSIDER THIS YOUR GAVEL

Officer Kingman didn't respond, not right away. As if he was gathering himself up for something important and wanted to get it right. When he did finally speak, he sounded calm and confident. "I may be a fool, Mr. Bragg, and it's true that I earn my living as a janitor, but I know something you don't."

"Oh, I doubt that."

"I know this nation still stands," Kingman said. "We've suffered a terrible blow, caused by some force of nature we don't fully understand, but the Constitution is still in force, and this is still America, and we'll deal with it, whatever it is."

"And you know this how? You read it on a Cracker Jack box?"

Kingman came right back at him. "When I volunteered to be a policeman, I raised my right hand and swore to uphold the law and act for the good of

49

the people. As a sworn officer I also received instruction on emergency response." He hesitated, then seemed to come to a decision. "This is supposed to be confidential, but I was given a special communication device—a kind of crystal radio—to be used in the event of disaster. That device has been silent since New Year's Eve. I assumed that it, too, had failed, but early this morning I finally received a message from the emergency response team for the state of New Hampshire."

"You're a liar!" Bragg erupted. "Radios don't work. Everybody knows that!"

"This one does. It's an old crystal set and doesn't require power."

"Prove it!"

For the first time since Webster Bragg and his bully sons swaggered into the town hall, Reggie Kingman actually smiled. "I asked about you, Mr. Bragg, and they told me not to worry. They said you have a lot of strange, hateful ideas about the world, but in America that's allowed. You can think what you like."

Bragg jerked his bearded chin out, addressing the crowd. "Oh yeah? Here's what I think. I think it's time to choose. Time for this town to pick a strong leader with strong ideas. Time for that leader to decide who can be trusted and who can't. And yes, it's time to identify the weak and the weak-minded and shove them out of the nest. I pledge to do that. I pledge to keep us safe. You have my word."

"What does that mean, 'shove them out of the nest'?" Kingman demanded.

"Hard decisions will have to be made," Bragg said, looking cunning. "Only the strong will survive what is to come. Those of us who planned for the dark times, we can't be expected to share our precious resources with those who didn't."

Officer Kingman shook his head. "You are entitled to that opinion, Mr. Bragg, but I disagree. Unlike you, I don't have any answers as to what the future might hold. All I can promise is this: If we look out for one another, nobody starves, nobody freezes. Stick together and we survive, the weak and strong alike."

"Pitiful," Bragg said, shaking his head in disgust. "You have proved my point. You're not fit to run a mop, let alone a town."

Somebody started banging on an empty aluminum bean pot. *Clang clang clang* with a big wooden spoon. It was the skinny old man, the one with the shakes. The one who looked like a faint breeze would blow him away. "Vote!" he called out in a surprisingly strong voice. "I call for a vote!"

Later on Mom told us the skinny old man was Hubert Brown, and he used to be the town moderator until he got Parkinson's disease and retired. Used to be a real stickler for the rules and going by the book, but was known to be fair. A lot of the older folks respected him. He opened his mouth to say something, but a fit of shakes bent him over double and made him drop the spoon.

He was all alone in a crowded room, shaking and unable to speak or stand upright. Then someone handed him the spoon and helped him close his fist around it, and get the shakes under control. "Consider this your gavel, Mr. Brown. Now what was it you were saying?"

The old man's head trembled like a leaf, but his voice was clear and strong. "All those who favor appointing Mr. Bragg to run the town of Harmony, stand up and say aye."

A few people stood, but not many, and they looked both defiant and a little ashamed of themselves.

"All those who favor sticking with Officer Kingman, stand up and say aye."

The ayes came as a roar.

"Kingman it is! This meeting is adjourned!"

11
BAMBI IN THE HALL

Too bad that wasn't how it ended. The good guys win, big cheer from the crowd, and everybody lives happily ever after. But nothing was simple that winter, and opinions kept changing. One day everybody seemed to be in agreement, that it made sense to let Officer Kingman be in charge of food and firewood and security. The next day rumors would run through Harmony like poison, darkening our minds, and what Bragg was saying about a great conspiracy almost seemed to make sense.

Not Becca, though. She was for Kingman and never wavered. "We can't be mean," she would say. "Being mean is just plain wrong."

Yeah, but. What about the Givens family, for example? Mr. and Mrs. Givens were bad drinkers, always fighting and complaining, and their two kids were even worse, being bullies and thieves. The entire family lived off the state, and naturally they didn't have so much as a can of tomato soup in the cupboards. Or any source of heat—chopping wood is way too difficult when you're drunk as a skunk by noon. So why should the rest of us have to chip in to help a family who couldn't be bothered to help themselves? And it's not like they were properly grateful for all the support. Old Man Givens was a foul-tempered drunk, and no matter what was provided, he always asked for more, and then cursed at those who helped.

Naturally they had a vicious pit bull, and that needed to be fed, too.

"I have a solution," Gronk announced with his pie-eating grin. "Feed the goony Givens family to the pit bull. Problem solved."

"If Bragg takes over, he just might do that."

"Let him. Just for a day. My dad says he'd clean house."

"I thought your dad thought Bragg was a nut bar."

"My dad does think he's a nut bar. He was joking."

"You're sure?"

Gronk thought about it. "Pretty sure," he said.

Which made sense. No one was sure of anything, not even jokes. Food wasn't really a problem, not yet, but fighting the cold was getting old. First thing we were all hoping for was that the power would come back on, and everything would return to normal. Second was for a January thaw, or, failing that, a few days above freezing, so we could all catch a breath and save a little firewood.

Mr. Mangano said we were caught in a polar vortex, basically cold air blowing down from the North Pole. Which was not unusual for this time of year and had nothing to do with the massive flare or the geomagnetic event or whatever it was that caused the big dark. School had been canceled for the time being—too many kids were needed at home. Plus the school building was like a freezer box—but Mr. Mangano started holding informal classes at the town hall a few hours each day for anybody who could get there.

Our first project? Build and maintain a weather station. The usual weather module didn't work, of course, so our assignment was to "devise and explore more traditional options." Which meant using an old-fashioned mercury thermometer— Gronk found it in the barn behind his house—and a wind indicator made of wire with tinfoil vanes, and an aneroid barometer. Gronk called it the hemorrhoid barometer, and Mr. Mangano laughed and said, "You have that in common with a hemorrhoid, Gary—you're both pains in the butt, but at least you're funny."

Mr. Mangano said we were all suffering from aimless compass syndrome. He sort of meant it as a joke, but it was like Harmony no longer had a direction, or even an opinion that didn't keep changing. Like we were all trying to find magnetic north, but we couldn't because it no longer existed.

I know, I know—it didn't make sense. That was the problem—nothing really made sense. And when nothing makes sense, crazy ideas like Bragg's start to seem not so crazy after all.

Kingman made sure the town hall was heated and open to the public during the day. He said the suggestion came over his special crystal radio, from the state emergency people, who said it was important for every town to establish a central place to go and be neighborly, and that's why the wide front door was kept off the latch.

Every day a new update would arrive over the crystal radio, and Kingman would post it on the pinup board beside the door.

Mostly announcements like *New Hampshire residents unite to face difficult challenges* and *Federal Emergency Management Agency officials confirm that the massive power outage is under investigation by top scientists, and urge citizens to keep calm.*

Gronk's dad grumbled that he wouldn't believe a thing FEMA said until they showed up and shoveled his sidewalk. But even he got a kick out of the New Hampshire Emergency Task Force Tip of the Day:

Make somebody smile. It warms the heart if not the hearth.

"Happy talk," he said, but it made him smile, so I guess it worked.

Gronk and I happened to be in the town hall one afternoon, working on our weather station project, when we got an unexpected visitor. First thing we noticed was the cold breeze from the open door, and then came the clopping of hooves.

"Oh my cheese," Gronk said under his breath. "It's Bambi!"

The deer, which weighed maybe a hundred pounds, did not seem to be anywhere near as excited as we were. She clopped along between the tables and chairs, found an open space not too far from the stove, lay down with her long spindly legs folded, and promptly fell asleep.

"Bambi was a male," I pointed out. "That's a doe. A year or so old."

"What do we do?"

"Let her sleep, I guess."

"Someone will want to shoot it," Gronk said, very matter-of-fact.

He had a point. This is the north country and hunting is what we do. Moose, deer, turkey, duck, bear—you name it, we shoot it. Rifle, shotgun, musket, bow, whatever gets the job done. Food for the freezer.

"Yeah, but why bother?" I said. "We've got more venison than we can eat before it goes bad. Besides, I'm not going to tell anybody, are you?"

Gronk shrugged. "Guess not."

The deer stayed overnight and was waiting to leave when we opened the door early the next morning. Trotted lightly out of town, not in any particular hurry. Like it knew hunting season was over and assumed the rules would be enforced. Or maybe, Gronk said, it just needed a break from the cold.

Anyhow, it was kind of a cool thing. For a while I thought maybe the visiting deer was a sign that things would get better, that we could all get along.

Then Mom got sick, and everything changed.

12
WHAT MRS. ADLER SAID

In my dream I was watching TV. Weird but true. Can't remember what show it was, just that the TV was working and everything was back to normal. It was warm, too, summer warm—not woodstove warm—and I could smell fresh-cut grass and cotton candy.

It was such a comfortable dream that I didn't want it to stop, even with Becca shaking me as hard as she could.

"Charlie! Charlie, wake up! Something's wrong with Mom!"

When my brain finally figured out what she was saying, I swung out of bed and put my feet on a floor as cold as an ice rink. Which startled me the rest of the way awake because Mom had been getting up every morning at four a.m. and loading the stove so it was warm when me and Becca got up.

Every morning, never failed.

Becca was crying, which scared me. Really scared me. Because it reminded me of how we found out that Dad had been killed in a skiing accident. Mom waking us up and telling us something really bad had happened, and then both of us crying until we choked, refusing to believe her when she told us a storm had come up suddenly, and he had hit a tree and died.

But it didn't matter how much we wanted it not to have happened. It did happen, and there was nothing we could do to change it.

We found Mom curled up on the bathroom floor. She wasn't asleep or unconscious, exactly, but her eyes were unfocused, and her words were slurred, as if she'd been drinking.

Okay, I know what you're thinking, but Mom didn't drink alcohol, not ever.

"What's she trying to say?" Becca wanted to know, desperately. "I can't figure it out. Charlie, figure it out, please please please."

I knelt beside Mom and leaned close. She was trying to say something but it sounded like baby talk, *ga ga ga*. Which totally freaked me out. It's stupid, but more than anything I wanted to ignore what was happening and pretend it was summertime and the TV was on.

When I tried to get up, Mom's hand locked around my wrist. She wanted me to lean closer.

"Nah me adah," Mom said, struggling to speak, her eyes rolling. "Nah me adah."

"Nah me adah?" I repeated to Becca.

My sister's eyes lit up. "Naomi Adler! Of course! She wants us to get Mrs. Adler!"

We covered Mom with blankets, because the floor was so cold, and I held her hands for dear life while Becca put on her snowmobile suit and went out to fetch Mrs. Adler.

An hour later Mom was in bed and sleeping soundly. Mrs. Adler took one look at her, checked the medicine cabinet, and then counted the pills in a medicine bottle.

"I was worried this might happen," she told us. "Are you aware that your mother has a form of type 2 diabetes? Okay. Of course you are. So you know she takes medication that helps regulate her blood sugar. Your mother picked up her prescription a day or so before the store burned. Wasn't only the food and sundries burned, it was the pharmacy, too. Anyhow, it looks like Emma was trying to stretch her prescription. Taking one pill every other day instead of every day. And it caught up with her."

"Is she going to be okay?"

As the manager of the Superette, Mrs. Adler was famous for telling it like it was, even if it hurt someone's feelings. No sugarcoating anything. Her store was gone, turned into frozen charcoal, but Mrs. Adler hadn't changed.

"I don't know," she told us. "I hope she'll be okay, but I'm not a doctor. I'm a licensed pharmacy assistant, which means I can pass along medication in consultation with a pharmacist. That was by phone, to the hospital pharmacy in Concord."

"But you know stuff," Becca said, begging. "Tell us what to do."

Mrs. Adler sighed. "I know enough to know that Emma can only do so much to regulate her blood sugar by managing her diet and so on. Her condition is quite serious, and she needs her medication."

"How long will her pills last, if she takes one every day like she's supposed to?"

Mrs. Adler held up the bottle. "You can count it yourself, to make sure. But I make it nineteen pills."

Nineteen pills. Nineteen days and counting.

13
THE RETURN OF BARF MAN

It's amazing what you can forget when you don't
want to think about it. Later Becca told me she had
been worried all along about Mom not having
enough pills. Not me. Maybe that was on purpose.
Ever since Dad died, Becca had worried Mom
would die, too. Again, not me. I refused to think
about it, because thinking about something bad
might make it more likely to happen. Which was
stupid, but that's how my brain works.

Anyhow, bottom line, I had to think about it
now. No choice. It wasn't like she'd die the moment
she ran out of medication. Being really careful with
her diet would help Mom keep her blood sugar
balanced for a while. Avoiding stress, that would
help, too. But the medication kept her stable over
the long run, so we needed to find more pills for
her, that's all there was to it.

But how? The nearest real pharmacy was fifty miles away, down through the forests and the mountains. In the dead of winter, all snowed in like we were, it might as well be a thousand miles.

Then an idea clicked on like a beautiful lightbulb.

It took a while to get in to see King Man. We didn't have a police station in Harmony, and the volunteer police officer didn't get an office or anything, so he was running his kingdom out of the old firehouse.

"King Man," that's what Gronk had started calling him, ever since Reggie Kingman won the vote at the town meeting. Gronk was joking, of course, but it was sort of true, because trying to see Kingman was like waiting in line at a royal palace or something. Not that the old firehouse was much of a palace. More like a dinky garage with a useless fire truck taking up most of the space. In the back was a small, windowless room that reminded me of the custodian's closet at school. Maybe that's why Kingman chose it. His throne was a swivel chair, and his crown was a knitted wool hat with earflaps, because the old potbelly stove barely kept the place above freezing.

King Man's special crystal radio that connected us to the outside world? It sat there on display, shiny and black as an ancient insect, in a wire cabinet over his desk. No microphone or speakers, just an old-fashioned headset and an antique-looking telegraph key wired up to a shortwave radio antenna.

Lucky for us, King Man knew Morse code. Learned it when he was a Boy Scout and still had the merit badge to prove it.

A bunch of people were waiting to see him, mostly to complain about the firewood tax. King Man had imposed a tax, amounting to half a cord per household, to provide for those who didn't have enough, and to keep the fire burning for the geezers he had installed in Moulton House.

From what I could tell, everybody in line thought it was a great idea, making sure nobody froze to death, but they all had a good excuse for why they shouldn't have to give up quite so much firewood. And it seemed like most of them were still grumbling when they left. Or complaining how it wasn't fair that Webster Bragg refused to contribute when everyone knew he had more wood pellets than anyone else.

Being the king didn't look like much fun, that's for sure.

"Charlie Cobb," he said when I finally got in the door. "To what do I owe the pleasure?"

The smile faded from his eyes as he heard that Mom might run out of medicine.

"I'm so sorry," he said. "I wish there was something I could do. Truly, I do."

"What about your radio thing? Telegraph a signal code to the emergency people. This is an emergency, right?"

King Man looked a little sick to his stomach. "Charlie, I'm sorry, but it doesn't work like that. The, um, connection is more of a general information

65

thing, and operation is restricted. They're not running a delivery service."

The little office was cool enough so we could see our breath, but for some reason those two words, *delivery* and *service*? They made my face hot, and my brain, too. "Can't you at least try? Ask and see what they say."

He hesitated, fiddling with one of his earflaps, and for a moment he looked more like Barf Man the custodian than King Man the ruler of Harmony. "Sure, sure. I'll ask, Charlie, but I know what the response will be. There must be hundreds, maybe thousands, of people in the north country who are low on medication."

"They could at least tell us where to find some!"

"Um, yeah. Um, possibly."

" 'Um, yeah'! This is my mom's life at stake, and all you can say is 'um, yeah'? What kind of king are you if you won't help!"

"Huh?" He looked startled. "In the first place, I'm not any kind of king, believe me. I am a facilitator of food and firewood. And I didn't say I wouldn't help. I'm just suggesting that what you request may be impossible."

"You're not even going to try!" I started to stomp out of that cold little room.

"Charlie, don't go away mad. I'll transmit the request, okay? See what happens. But maybe we're worried about nothing. Maybe the power will be restored soon, and the roads will get plowed, and your mother can drive down to Concord and fill her own prescription. Nineteen days, why not? Plenty of time. There's always hope."

That hit me like a shock, for some reason. A shock of hope. "Is that what it says on the emergency radio? That it'll be over soon?"

He hesitated, glancing away from me. "Um, no. Not exactly. The situation, well, there's an ongoing evaluation of the situation, and, ah, bottom line, no one can say when power will be restored. We've, ah, been advised to get through the winter as best we can, on our own for the time being. One day at a time, Charlie."

One day at a time. Which wasn't very many if all you had was nineteen of them.

14
NOT ANOTHER WORD

Night was so very dark. Not the kind of night we were used to before the lights went out. Back when streetlights touched the sky, and houses and buildings were alive with artificial illumination, and the world seemed to breathe with a warm glow that we didn't even notice because it was always there.

This was a much darker place.

There were patches of stars visible that particular evening, the night I found out King Man was lying. But the light from the stars didn't seem to get all the way to the ground. I could feel my feet inside my boots, attached to my legs, but I couldn't see them; they were part of the dark.

Don't fall, I told myself. *If you fall, the dark of night will swallow you up and never let you go.*

The side door to the old firehouse groaned as I pushed it open, letting in a gust of frozen air.

Black dark. Couldn't see a thing.

Out of my pocket came a nub of candle and a small box of wooden matches. Matches were precious, nearly as valuable as candles or kerosene lanterns. My fingers were as numb as Popsicles, but I managed to light the candle, and the darkness backed up a step or two. The dull gleam of the useless fire truck reflected the flicker of the candle flame, and me holding it.

I knew exactly where to go. The candle wasn't the only thing in my pockets. There was a big brawny screwdriver in case King Man had padlocked his office door. But when I got there, the door was open, and the potbelly stove glowed faintly.

King Man cleared his throat. "Have a seat, Charlie. Take a load off."

My heart pounded like the high striker at the Lancaster Fair.

"Thought you might drop by," he said. "You had that look in your eye."

Too dim to see his expression, but his voice was smiling. A chair creaked as he leaned back, waiting for me to respond.

"I came for the radio," I blurted.

"Got it right here on my desk," he said softly. "I've been listening for the last hour or so, like I do most every night. That's when reception is supposed to be the best."

My eyes had adjusted enough so I could just make out the radio gear on his desk and the old headphones hanging around his neck.

"You going to let them know my mom needs medicine?"

"Sorry, Charlie. I can't."

Disgusted, I blurted out, "If you won't try, I will!"

"Charlie, please."

"I don't know Morse code but I know SOS. Three dots, three dashes, three dots. Maybe they'll hear it. Maybe they'll come."

"Uh-huh," he said slowly. "Let me share something with you, Charlie, about this radio. It's an old crystal set I built long ago, when I was about your age. You know anything about crystal sets? No reason you would. Thing about a crystal set, it doesn't require power to detect radio waves. See this part? Wire coiled around a cardboard toilet paper tube. One end attached to the antenna, here, the other to this little bit of crystal mineral. This? They call it a cat's whisker. A tiny sliver of metal that just barely tickles the piece of mineral. And that's all there is to it. It works because the radio waves themselves create just enough power to make themselves heard."

I didn't know what to say, or why he was telling me stuff about his old radio. It's not as if I was going to build one of my own.

"Have a listen, Charlie. Tell me what you hear."

He handed me the headphones. Unlike the headphones I had at home, there was no cushiony foam, and I had to hold them close to my ears to make them fit.

"I can't hear anything," I told him.

"Keep listening. You have young ears. I'm going to very slowly move this piece along the coil, which is the same as going up and down a radio dial. If you hear a signal, let me know, and I'll hold that position."

After a while my ears sort of adjusted, and I could just make out a low, distant static. Sounded very small and a million miles away.

In the flicker of the candlelight, King Man studied me intently as his hand deftly adjusted the old crystal set, searching for a signal.

Nothing but static.

We went up and down that coil.

Nothing.

Nothing.

Nothing.

Finally I took the headphones off and dropped them on his desk. "Nobody there," I admitted. "Why did you say there was? Why did you lie?"

King Man sighed. "I keep hoping I'll hear something, or someone, but I suspect if there are others out there—and I firmly believe there are—they have the same problem I do."

"What problem? Making stuff up?"

"A crystal set is passive, Charlie. We can listen, but we can't broadcast. Even the simplest and most primitive method of producing a signal—a spark-gap generator, which is what I have right here, this old telegraph key—it requires power. Enough electrical current to jump a gap. And that we don't have. I suspect no one else has it, either. Hence the radio silence."

"That still doesn't explain why you lied."

He shrugged. "Because I wanted it to be true? To believe that someone out there was taking

71

charge, fixing whatever broke, urging us to take care of each other? It's about hope, Charlie. That's one thing we need more than firewood or food. Without it, the Braggs of the world will take over. The haters will win."

"Or you made it up so you could be king!" I said, tears of anger hot in my eyes.

"Maybe," he admitted. "I'm not a perfect man. Far from it."

"What about Mr. Mangano? Does he know?"

"We haven't discussed it, but I'm sure he does. Can't fool Joe, not about something like this."

"And now you want me to lie, too. To keep your secret."

Before answering he opened the stove door with a pair of tongs and added a small chunk of wood. In the brighter light he looked old, with hooded eyes like some ancient bald eagle, and he sounded old, too, his voice as creaky as the chair he was sitting in.

"This has been a long, hard winter even before the power failed," he said. "People get desperate, Charlie. They do desperate things. I was desperate enough to make up a story to make people feel a little better. Webster Bragg and his boys are so desperate for the world to end that they burned down the Superette, and they'll do worse, given the chance. It's not fair, Charlie, but you're going to have to choose. Me or Bragg? What will it be?"

I stood up, tightening the hood on my parka.

"Charlie?"

I left without saying another word.

*   *   *

Okay, I'll admit it, I didn't know what to do about King Man. It was so messed up. Should I tell everybody he was a fake? That he lied about his special crystal radio? Did I really have to choose between him and the awful Mr. Bragg?

But the thing that really freaked me was this: How were we ever going to find the medicine Mom needed?

All of it whirled around inside my head so much that I didn't know what to think. Except that I couldn't tell Mom. King Man was right about one thing: people needed hope. And I needed a plan.

If only I knew what to do.

Eventually I fell asleep.

15
THE JUMPED-UP JANITOR

The King Man situation got worse the very next day, and this time Becca was there to see it. She was helping out the geezers at Moulton House, preparing food and melting snow for water, when Webster Bragg strolled into the place with a tight little smile showing through his chin beard.

Like the Big Bad Wolf, Becca told me and Gronk later.

Didn't bother to say hello, or why he was there, just plopped onto a stool by an open fireplace and warmed his hands. As if he owned the place, Becca said. She asked what he wanted and he said, "I want people to wake up and smell the coffee." When Becca asked if that meant he would like a cup of coffee, he looked at her with his weird pale eyes and shook his head. "Are you a retard, child? Brain damaged? No? Then why are you wasting your time in this dump?"

Take it from me, my sister isn't usually at a loss for words, but apparently she was still processing *retard*, a word she never uses, and the best she could come up with was "I'm lending a hand."

"You want to lend a hand? Move into my compound, work in the kitchen with the rest of the females, under my protection. Plenty of heat, and three squares a day. You'll be safe, and you won't have to worry about the world beyond the gate, because that's my job. Think about it. Meanwhile, I'm requisitioning this firewood."

"You can't do that!"

"Watch me," he said, and began loading chunks of wood into his arms.

Later Mom said Becca should have come straight home, but my sister has a mind of her own, and she decided to alert King Man to what was going on.

It wasn't until she was outside that she realized the Moulton place was surrounded by Bragg's sons, who had toboggans ready to load with the firewood they were intending to steal.

Reggie Kingman responded right away. Put on his cop hat, marched over from the fire station, and ordered Bragg to cease and desist or he would be arrested for unlawful taking.

Bragg sneered at him. "Unlawful? You attempt to put an unlawful tax on my firewood, and I respond by seizing yours. That's *my* law."

King Man appeared flustered, or maybe it was embarrassment on behalf of the old geezers, who were too weak and out of it to defend themselves.

"That tax was to help those who couldn't help themselves," he said. "To get us all through the winter. It was the right thing to do."

Bragg scoffed. "Seemed right to you because you're almost as noodle-brained as these takers," he said, gesturing at the elderly residents.

"Takers?"

"Can't fend for themselves so they take, take, take. Trying to bring us all down to their level. Times like these, the strong have to shed the weak. Those confined to wheelchairs, deaf and demented, pooping in diapers, what good are they? What use? It would be a kindness to put these folks outside, let nature take its course."

"You wouldn't dare!"

Bragg chuckled, looking down his long nose at Reggie Kingman. "Won't be me, wheeling them out. No, I'll leave that up to you. Changing dirty nappies is about all you're good for. I'm betting you won't draw that sidearm and risk these useless takers getting shot in the cross fire."

"You'd do that? Open fire on innocent, helpless people?"

"I'll do whatever it takes to accomplish my mission."

"Robbing the weak, is that your mission?" Kingman asked, as if he really wanted to know.

Bragg smiled, satisfied. He'd been waiting all along to have the last word. "Truth? I don't really care about the firewood, although it will come in handy. This isn't about firewood or the feebleminded. My mission is to show the so-called citizens of Harmony exactly what you really are. A jumped-up janitor. A toilet-swabbing loser. A maker of empty promises and false hopes. A lawman who can't enforce the law."

At a signal from Bragg, his sons swarmed into Moulton House and took every stick of firewood. Some of the old geezers understood what was happening and cried out. Becca tried her best, but they couldn't be comforted. And faced with heavily armed thugs, what did King Man do?

He did nothing.

I was expecting Mom to be as disgusted as me when she heard the story, which was all over town, and the cause of a lot of speculation about whether or not King Man's day was done. But instead of being disgusted, she took his side, more or less. And she didn't like it when I snorted in disagreement, not one bit.

"Don't you dare judge him, Charlie Cobb! Reggie's doing the best he can in a terrible situation. His job is to protect those who can't protect themselves, and that's what he did, at the expense of his own pride."

"He backed down, Mom! He let Bragg get away with it!"

Mom opened her mouth to respond—something sharp, no doubt—and then thought better of it. After a deep breath she resumed in her listen-to-teacher voice. "Sometimes backing down is the best thing to do, like it or not. Your sister was right there when it happened! What if they'd opened fire? She might have been killed!"

I hadn't thought about that, which only made me madder. I wanted to tell her about the useless radio and the fake messages of hope, and how King Man wasn't doing anything to help find her medicine. But I couldn't do it, not and look Mom in the eye.

Besides, I wasn't doing anything about it, either. Which meant I wasn't any braver or smarter than a jumped-up janitor, right?

Right?

Seventeen days and counting.

16
TRACKS IN THE SNOW

Not everybody agreed with Mom, not by a long shot. I overheard Gronk's mother yakking with Mrs. Adler, and they were saying if Kingman couldn't or wouldn't stand up to Bragg, then maybe the town needed to find a new leader. And there were even those who thought maybe it was a mistake not to have voted for Bragg when they had the chance—not so much because they agreed with his conspiracy and racial theories, but because if elected he might be inclined to share his stockpile of supplies.

"Reggie is a good man, but he's out of his depth," someone said. "If he wants to handle a bully like Webster Bragg, he's going to have to do more than recite the Pledge of Allegiance."

When Kingman posted the latest message from his fake radio, a lot of folks shook their heads.

*New Hampshire's Special Emergency Response
Team suggests that for the duration of the power outage,
citizens band together to assist those who can't help
themselves.*

"Like we didn't know that?" Mrs. Adler said,
sounding disgusted. "We need help, not homilies!"

Even when it became known that Reggie had
moved the geezers from Moulton House into his
own home, some took it as a sign of weakness.

"That won't work, not in the long run. He'll run
out of firewood that much sooner, and then they'll
all freeze to death. What's he trying to prove? That
he's better than us?"

The talk got so harsh I almost changed my mind
about King Man being a liar and a loser. But not
quite. That didn't happen until later in the afternoon, when the old man of the mountains skied
into Harmony, easy as you please. If you don't
count the five armed men who followed at a distance, aiming rifles at his head.

Me and Gronk were at the weather station when it
happened.

The sun was out and it was warm enough so
our breath hardly showed. Mr. Mangano had a
theory that the thaw everybody was praying for
had finally arrived. If he was right, and the high
pressure held, we might get as much as a week
above freezing. Which is why we were check-
ing the barometer every hour and seeing if
the breeze kept steady from the south, warming the

air and giving us all a break from the bone-snapping cold.

Gronk was the first to see what was going on.

"Get ready to duck!" he said, his eyes going wide.

Coming down the middle of Main Street, gliding smooth and steady, was a man on cross-country skis. An older-looking dude with a long chin, a thin hawk nose, and big square teeth. Fastened to a harness around his shoulders was a long leash tied to a light sled. The sled was neatly packed with duffel bags and a sleeping bag. This old dude, long and lean, was moving like a machine, hardly having to lift a ski to keep his momentum, and the sled followed just behind, neat as you please.

What he didn't know was this: five masked men were tracking him like a rabbit in the snow. Full winter camo, ski masks covering everything but their eyes. Moving silently, sighting down their rifles. Not saying a word, as if afraid they might spook their quarry into skiing faster, becoming even more of a moving target.

Something about seeing a man being hunted, it kind of froze my brain as well as my feet. Gronk, too. Both of us holding our breath and dreading the snap of a rifle shot.

Unaware he was being tracked, the skier swooped up to our little weather station and planted his poles and said, "Harmony, I presume?"

We nodded like doofuses, our eyes locked on the men with rifles behind him.

"Haven't been through in a while," the skier said affably. "Looks different buried under six feet of snow."

Through his frozen grin, Gronk said, "Mister, you better not move."

The man couldn't turn that easily, planted on skis, but he managed to swivel his head just enough to see what was going on behind him.

"Oh my," he said. "Is this a welcoming party?"

One of the riflemen lifted the ski mask from his face. Webster Bragg, looking very satisfied. "We've got you dead to rights," he said, his strange pale eyes glinting. "Trespassing on our territory. Spying on us."

"Hey, I'm just passing through," the skier said, startled by the accusation.

"Not likely," Bragg said dismissively. "Who sent you? The UN? The feds?"

"Sent me? Nobody sent me. I'm heading to Claremont. Got family there."

Bragg spat casually, just missing the skier. "That's fifty miles west of here. You expect us to believe that?"

The man glanced at where the spit landed and stood taller. Looked younger, too, the way his eyes started to hold courage. "Believe what you like, sir. The trail is downhill, and I'm on skis, case you hadn't noticed. Covered twenty-eight miles since sunrise, and expect to find Claremont before the sun goes down. I'm a mountain man, born and raised. Fifty miles is no big thing if the weather holds."

"And if it doesn't?"

"I'll dig in, wait it out."

"Why should I believe you?" Bragg said.

The skier shrugged. "Because I'm not in the habit of lying. Let me pass."

Bragg said slyly, "So how'd you find your way without a compass?"

The skier shook his head. "Don't need a compass. I've been following this road, and I will follow one road or another to my destination. My trail has been blazed by the New Hampshire Department of Transportation, and all the road and highway departments of all the good towns and villages between here and there. Satisfied?"

"Not hardly," Bragg said. "I say you're a spy sent to betray us. Step out of those skis and come with me!"

"No, sir, I will not."

I don't know what would have happened if King Man hadn't shown up at that moment. He seemed to come out of nowhere, slipping between Bragg and the man on skis, an ungloved hand gripping the pistol in his polished holster.

"Mr. Bragg, I am asking you to step away. I know this man, and he's no spy."

The skier said, "Reggie? Reggie Kingman? I'll be darn."

It was all Webster Bragg could do not to stamp his feet in frustration. "This man is my prisoner. He's a stranger among us and must be interrogated."

King Man said, "No need. His name is Alden

Remick. Lives out in the boonies north of here. I happen to know he has a daughter living in Claremont with his grandchildren."

The skier chuckled. "Reggie and I used to belong to the same shooting club, back in the day."

"Shooting club?"

The skier looked amused. "Didn't you know? Reginald Kingman was the best pistol shot in the state. Might still be, for all I know."

Bragg backed up a few steps. "Is that right?"

So there it was, finally. A genuine standoff. The King Man waited to see what Bragg would do, and Bragg waited for him, both of them tense as coiled springs, ready to draw and fire.

Gronk said later it was a good thing a sparrow didn't fart, or the guns would have been blazing. As it turned out, Reggie Kingman was the first to take the pressure off by moving his hand slightly away from his holster. "Tell you what, Web. If this man turns out to be a spy, you have my permission to shoot me. I won't defend myself."

Bragg looked from the old skier to King Man and back. "I have your word on that?"

"You do."

Bragg thought about it, then jerked his hairy chin at the skier. "Be on your way, pilgrim. Let them know we will defend ourselves against those who would take what is ours, be it freedom or firewood."

"Huh?" the skier said.

"Get out of here while the getting's good."

So it all ended without a shot fired. Bragg and his boys faded back into the woods, and the skier departed, towing his little sled, leaving nothing behind but thin tracks in the snow.

Thin tracks in the snow, and an idea that could change everything.

17
VENISON JERKY

Whatever you might think about what I did, please don't blame it on Gronk. Yes, he agreed to help me. Yes, he could have tattled on me and he didn't. But he did what a true friend does: he trusted me to do what was right, even if it seemed wrong at the time. He told me so, too. Said I was crazier than a hound with a nose full of porcupine quills. He thought my plan was dangerous and possibly just plain stupid.

"Maybe it is, but it's the only plan I've got."

"What about bears?" he wanted to know.

"Hibernating."

"What about wolves?"

"You ever seen one?"

He shook his head.

"I have to do this, Gronk. You'd do the same if it was your mother."

"My dad would take care of it," he said, and then grimaced. "Sorry."

"Don't be sorry. Just lend me your best skis and enough jerky to get me there and back."

Because that was my plan. Ski mostly downhill to Concord while the weather was fair, find the hospital pharmacy that supplied the Superette, get enough medication to last until spring, then snow-shoe back up through the mountains to Harmony. Simple. If an old dude could cover twenty-eight miles in less than a day and make it look easy, so could I. Skiing down a snow-covered road, on a proper incline? Nothing to it. Before my father passed, me and Becca cross-country skied all the time and loved it. After, Mom burned Dad's equipment and refused to let us go. Told us her head would explode with worry, on account of what happened to Dad.

Now I was breaking that promise, but for a good reason. When her medication ran out, Mom could go into shock or slip into a coma. She might even die. And Becca couldn't stand it if she lost both parents. She'd go mental or worse. So I couldn't let that happen. No way.

If King Man couldn't help, I'd have to do it on my own.

That night was so weird, having supper with my family and not being able to tell them about my big plan. Mom was feeling better and that made Becca happy, but if they knew what I had in mind they'd have flipped out.

Well, Becca might understand, but not Mom. There's no doubt in my mind that she would forbid me from going down the mountain, even if her life depended on it. Which it did. So I kept my trap shut for as long as I could stand it, and then when I did speak up, I told a lie.

"Mom? Can I go over to the Smalls' after supper? Gronk and I are working on a weather project for Mr. Mangano."

That was partly true, about the weather project, but the intention, as my mother would say, was to hide the truth. Mom was like a maniac about telling the truth. I asked her once if lying was as bad a sin as murder, and she said lying murdered trust, so almost.

"Gary is always welcome in this home," Mom reminded me. "He can come over here for the evening."

"Mr. Small is going to show us how to make a better wind indicator."

She looked at me in a way that made me think she knew something was up. "Okay then. Do the Smalls have a windup clock?"

"Yeah."

"Be home by nine. The stove will hold until then."

"I, um, I'm glad you're better, Mom," I said to hide my nervousness.

"You children are not to worry. Is that understood?"

Becca caught my eye—she'll always be worried, that's who she is—but we both nodded and promised not to worry, and a few minutes later I was out the door and heading to Gronk's.

*   *   *

"Thermal underwear?"

"Check."

"Insulated ski boots?"

"Check."

"Extra-thick, superwicking socks?"

"Check."

"Full-face wind mask?"

"Check."

We were in the cellar, supposedly tending the pellet stove by the light of a kerosene lantern. Gronk handed me a carefully wrapped Ziploc bag, a big one. "Venison jerky. Enough to keep you alive for about a month."

"It'll only be a few days, but thanks. Yum yum."

"Think of it as Bambi steak," he said with a goofy grin.

"You're sick."

"I know, right? Okay, back to the list. You're taking my sleeping bag, period, no argument. Waterproof and good to fifty below."

I was planning to use my own, but Gronk insisted his was better. "Thanks."

"And my off-trail XCs with the super light poles."

"I'll get the skis back to you, Gronk. Promise."

He leaned forward, eyes glittering in the lantern light. "I don't care about the skis, you moron. You better come home in one piece or I'm finished, okay? Your mom will vote me off the island."

"Harmony isn't an island," I pointed out.

"You know what I mean. If it doesn't go right, we're both going to be in huge trouble, not just you."

"I'll be fine. Olympic cross-country racers cover fifty kilometers in two hours. That's like thirty miles. I've got all day to go fifty, most of it downhill."

"You're not an Olympic racer, Charlie. Far as I know you haven't skied in two years."

"I'll be following a road that's wider and safer and sloped better than any trail."

"I guess. What'll I say to Becca? She's going to hate me."

"I'm leaving her a note. She'll understand."

Gronk sighed. "This is so wacked, but you know what? It's a pretty cool thing you're doing."

Pretty cool, maybe. If it worked. If I made it back in time with the medicine. If I didn't get eaten by imaginary wolves. If I didn't freeze to death in a sudden blizzard, or get lost, or run into a tree like my father.

If, if, if.

I really hated that word.

18
A TERRIBLE SURPRISE

Dawn found me sneaking out of the house like a thief. Like a liar. Like a boy with something to hide. Totally aware of how upset my family would be when they found me gone, but doing it anyhow.

Couldn't be helped. I was on a mission. My mother would never have approved, but in my heart I knew what my father would say.

Go for it, Charlie boy.

Not because my father wanted me to take unnecessary or foolish risks—he wasn't that kind of dad—but because he would understand. I can't put it into words, but he just would, okay? I mean, what would you do if it was your mom?

I slipped into the shoulder straps of the loaded backpack. Snowshoes tied to the sleeping bag, check. Then I stepped into Gronk's skis, as I had rehearsed in my brain a million times. The bindings snapped over my boots with a soft click. I gripped the poles in my mittens and took a deep breath of the cold air.

I wasn't moving yet, so why was my heart racing?

Relax, Charlie. You'll feel better once you're on your way.

And you know what? By the time the sun had inched over the horizon, I was gone. On my way. Gliding down the shallow slope in the backyard, making an easy turn onto the snow-covered road, using the poles to pick up speed. *Shoosh . . . shoosh . . . shoosh*, making the snow talk. Getting into the rhythm, into the balance of the thing.

It felt so right I had to consciously slow myself down. Better to keep a steady pace than to cramp up or pull a muscle. This wasn't a race. I was in it for the long haul.

The first part of my plan was to get out of Harmony without attracting the attention of Webster Bragg and his sons. In their wacked minds they might think I was escaping behind enemy lines or whatever. Best thing, avoid them altogether. The Bragg compound was a couple of miles to the east of the main road out of town, so I looped to the west, away from that whole area, and luck was with me. I never saw a soul.

Air temperature was slightly above freezing. I could feel that in the skis, the way they glided over the snow, riding on a little layer of melt. So the fair weather was holding, like Mr. Mangano said it might, at least for now.

As the pale winter sun rose, the shadow line of night backed up the snow-covered mountainsides, lifting my spirits. Coming off the loop and onto the main road, I was greeted by a forest of birches bowing like ballet dancers under skirts of ice, as if to see me off.

You're doing the right thing.

I hoped that was true. At the moment my mission was to keep moving, covering ground. The first long stretch of road, blanketed in at least five feet of snow, was downhill, and mostly I let the skis do the work. Tucking the poles under my elbows, crouching over the skis as the miles melted away.

Last time I was on this road it was in the Ford Explorer, with Mom and Becca, and I wasn't really paying attention. Why would I? You had to get somewhere, you got in a car and drove. Didn't even think about it. Now, with no compass or GPS, the only map was the one in my head. I could picture it, the place where the long road to Harmony met the highway, just beyond the gap in the mountains. My plan was to get there well before noon.

I was making really good time, eating up the miles, when I came around a long, spruce-lined curve and saw the first dead body hanging in a tree.

19
MILES TO GO BEFORE I SLEEP

The tail section of the airplane poked out of a massive snowdrift like a hand saluting heaven. Most of the wreckage lay broken and buried, forming snowy lumps as big as trucks, but the tailpiece soared over my head. Not a small airplane, that's for sure. And not military, which was the first thing that came to mind, because of Aunt Beth in the Air National Guard. Could be one of the regional jets that flew between Manchester and Quebec. Must have lost power and tried to land on the highway. Clipped the trees and broke up, spewing passengers, then got covered by the blizzard. Except for the victims flung into the trees.

Three dead bodies, draped like empty gloves over the bare branches, and coated in layers of ice that glinted in the noonday sun. Gronk has a joke: Where do little ice cubes come from? Popsicles and Momsicles.

Popsicles and Momsicles. Couldn't unthink that, no matter how hard I tried. Because there might be more bodies buried under the snow, maybe right under my skis. That should be scary or creepy, but instead it just made me feel incredibly sad.

Whatever had happened, it must have taken place moments after the event or pulse, or whatever it was. It was so weird to think that one minute we were all amazed by the shape-shifting lights in the sky, and the next moment everything changed. Lights went out, motors stopped, planes fell to Earth. People died.

Don't stop, don't look back. There's nothing for you here.

And so I pushed on. Down the snow-blanketed highway, down the mountain, down and down. Gronk's skis slipping over the crusted snow with a sound like a big cat purring.

An hour or so after the sun peaked—just a guess, because I didn't have a watch—I stopped, unclipped the skis, and took a break. My thighs ached, and my ankles were a little sore, but despite that, I felt amazingly good. No sign of cramps or blisters or anything. Air temp was definitely above freezing, and my clothes kept me plenty warm.

My plan was working. A few thoughts of Mom and Becca blipped in my head—they'd be going nuts with worry about now—but I forced them out. No time for regrets. I had a task to accomplish. And the task right then, right that instant, was to eat something to keep up my strength.

I retrieved the venison jerky from my backpack and slid open the big Ziploc bag. The smell of smoked meat hit me. Whew! Gronk was right, there must be enough for a month, because each thin slice took a long time to chew and was very filling.

Truth is, I'm not a big fan of jerky, so it helped to be hungry. Even so, I couldn't finish the third piece and finally tossed it to the ground. Left it for the squirrels or the birds or whatever.

Big mistake, but I didn't know that at the time.

I hefted the pack up on my shoulders and stepped into the skis. Pushed off with my poles, on the move again.

No idea how far I had to go to get there before nightfall. There were no recognizable landmarks on the long, swooping curves of the highway, at least not recognizable to me. The green highway signs indicated towns and villages I had never bothered to notice when we cruised by in our comfortable SUV. Now and then I glimpsed a distant silo poking out of the snow, or a cluster of homes with smoking chimneys, but I wasn't tempted to investigate.

Stick to the highway, that was my plan. *Ignore anything that looks like a shortcut, because you might lose your way. Give a wide berth to the big, frozen lumps that must be abandoned cars and trucks, buried under the snow. Think about where you're going, not where you've been, and don't stop until you get there.*

Push, stride, *purr*.
Push, stride, *purr*.

Not too fast, not too slow. Keep it going. Keep moving, Charlie Cobb, and you'll get there, you'll make it.

Miles to go before I sleep. Who said that? Must have been Becca, some poem or song she likes.

Don't think about Becca, don't think about Mom, don't think about the wrecked plane or the frozen dead. Don't think about anything but where you're heading. Stay on track, stick with the plan.

Push, stride. Push, stride. *Glide when you can, push when you can't.*

Onward, onward, never look back—unless something catches up.

And then it did.

Coyotes.

A whole pack of them, whining for my blood.

20
HUNGRY YELLOW EYES

Okay, maybe it wasn't a whole pack, but there were at least four coyotes on my trail. Hunting me, that was obvious. Thin and hungry—starving, it looked like—with mangy, reddish-brown coats and long snouts and yellow eyes. And teeth. Lots of teeth.

The closest coyote was about thirty feet away. Weighed maybe forty pounds. He was the leader, and the others yipped and whined as they cowered behind him, as if asking for instructions, or permission to attack.

Coyotes will run down a deer. Why not a human?

I faced them with a ski pole in my hands, ready to fend them off, or die trying, which seemed a distinct possibility.

First thought: *Wish I had a gun*. Could have gotten hold of a hunting rifle easy, but guns are heavy and I was traveling light. Mostly I didn't want to give Bragg and his boys an excuse to shoot me. And the fact is, these coyotes were so desperate I'm not sure they'd have cared if one of them got shot. Before I had a chance to aim a second time, they'd be on me, tearing me to pieces.

Make some noise, Charlie. Show 'em who's boss.

I lunged with the point of the ski pole, screaming. Not words, just screaming.

The coyotes lowered their hindquarters and crept backward, tails down, whining and yipping. But they didn't run away. And the boss coyote backed up the least, and very soon crept forward.

Low to the ground, ready to charge.

Fool. That piece of jerky.

Of course. Their starving noses had picked up the scent, and it was driving them crazy.

"HA!" I shouted, stabbing the pole in the air. "GET BACK! YOU WANT IT? I GOT IT!"

But instead of backing away, all four coyotes dropped their shrunken bellies to the snow, crouching.

Waiting.

They were thinking. Trying to figure me out. Calculating how to get me down without getting hurt. How to tear me apart and find the source of the smell.

Slowly, keeping one hand on the outthrust pole, I shifted the pack from my shoulder. Slipped my hand inside.

Coyotes are famous for being smart, and the hungry yellow eyes studied my every move. *Does the human have a weapon? Can he kill us before we kill him? How do we get what we want and stay alive?*

Inside the pack I carefully opened the Ziploc bag and dug into it, filling my fist with about half the contents.

"Good doggy," I said in a good-doggy voice. Which was probably stupid. These weren't dogs. Not even close.

"Good doggy."

They lifted their noses, baring their teeth.

I flung the handful of jerky outward, as far as it would go, scattering slices of smoked venison over the snow. Boss coyote growled a warning: the food was his, they were not to touch it until he ate his fill.

The three smaller coyotes held still for a heartbeat, but they couldn't help themselves. They were starving. Emitting little yips of unbearable excitement, they attacked the jerky slices, gobbling up chunks of snow and meat, shrieking at the others to stay away, *this is mine mine mine.*

The boss coyote hadn't moved. His eyes burned with fear and hatred. He knew I had more in my pack and he wanted it, every bite, all for himself.

He charged. I'd never seen anything so fast, but I was already in motion, triggered by the hunger in his eyes.

My hand swept out of the pack, tossing the Ziploc high in the air.

The boss coyote leapt, caught it in his mouth in midair, and before he hit the ground the other three were on him, fighting for the bag.

Go. Go. Go.

Now was my chance, while they were distracted, fighting among themselves. I jammed the poles in the snow and pushed with all my might, heading down the slope. Striding with everything I had, picking up speed. Scared to death they'd run me down and tear me to pieces like that bag of jerky.

But they didn't. And when I finally dared to turn my head and look, the highway was empty behind me, and the only thing I could hear was the blood pounding in my ears.

Never skied so hard in my life, or so fast. And to tell the truth, I never felt so alive.

21
TRAY BON, HE SAID

So I kept pushing as if my life depended on it, and maybe it did.

Pushing until my legs felt like rubber and my arms were wet spaghetti. And then I pushed some more, because the sun kept getting lower in the sky.

Truth is, I was chasing daylight. If worst came to worst I had Gronk's super-duper sleeping bag, but my plan didn't include sleeping out in the open. Not with packs of starving coyotes roaming around, and who knows what other creatures. Bobcats, possibly. Never heard of a bobcat hunting anything as big as a person, but if humans were acting crazy, why not animals, too?

I had no clear idea of how many miles yet to go. Made me wish I'd paid more attention the last time we drove down to the hospital, when Mom had an appointment at the clinic to check her blood levels and stuff. In my mind I saw us getting off the high-way at this big cloverleaf where the roads all merged. Mom pointing out the gold dome of the statehouse.

The hospital wasn't far from that exit. Less than a mile.

My plan was to get to the cloverleaf and then ask for directions. Concord is pretty big, so there was bound to be someone who knew where the hospital was, right?

Seemed as if I should be there already, but there was no sign of a city. Just trees and skinny forests on both sides of the highway, mile after mile. Sometimes the trees cleared out for a mile or two, and I was striding through fields of snow that threatened to submerge the highway. The downward incline had become very slight. Couldn't just crouch over my skis and glide, like when I first started out. I had to work for every yard.

Push, stride. Push, stride. The skis were no longer purring. Not enough speed.

Late in the day I got so exhausted it almost felt like I was skiing through a dream. Like the world was fading all around me, blending into the darkening sky, and the frozen trees were wriggling white fingers. Snow-laden spruce branches swayed in the wind, whispering, *What's your hurry? Take it easy, rest awhile.*

I thought of my father, downhill skiing on a beautiful bright winter day, when a freak snowstorm came on so thick and fast that he lost his way and hit a tree. Were voices calling him? What did they say? Did he listen?

So when I heard the voice in the distance, it was like part of my waking dream. The trees trying to fool me. Then it got louder, a long plaintive cry. "Haaaaallllllllllp! Haaaalllllllllllp!"

I stopped, planted my poles, and lifted the earflaps on my thick wool hat.

There it was again, but fainter, smaller. "Haalllp . . . haalllp."

Not the trees, and not a bird or a coyote. A human crying for help. Getting weaker with each cry.

I cupped my hands and shouted, "Where! Are! You!"

"Haalllp! Over here!"

A little stronger and even more urgent. The temperature was dropping quickly as the sun went down. I could feel it on my face and in my lungs. Cold and getting colder.

I pushed off the highway in the direction of the voice. There was an embankment along the road that had been obscuring my view. Probably made the voice harder to hear, too. When I got to the top of the rise the first thing I saw was a square flicker of yellow light. A lantern in a window. I could just make out the shape of a small house and a few slanted sheds and smell the aroma of a wood fire.

"HAAALLLP!"

He was there by the woodpile, half-buried in chunks of firewood. An old man in a parka with a fur hood. Inside the hood, a weathered, hatchet-shaped face with a white chin beard and worried eyes.

"Are you dere, you? Can't see too good. Broke my glasses, might be my leg, too."

"I'm here. Let me give you a hand."

"What's your name, you?"

"Charlie Cobb."

I stepped out of the skis, planted them in the snow, and helped him crawl out from under the collapsed woodpile. He was a skinny little guy, trembling with exertion, but with my help he managed to stand and test his leg.

"Not broke," he said. "Tray bon!"

I helped him limp to the little house, and when we pushed open the door an old woman began to keen, crying with joy to see him alive.

And that's how I met Pete Boncoeur and his sweet wife, Louise.

22
PROMISE YOU ME

Seeing an old geezer smother his wife with kisses, normally that would be extremely icky, but this was sort of okay, considering the circumstances. The wife, Louise, was confined to a wheelchair. She had been watching out the window when the woodpile collapsed on her husband, and thought he was a goner. Must have felt helpless, stuck in that chair.

Anyhow, they insisted I stay for dinner. And they didn't have to ask twice. Louise had a pot of stew warming on the woodstove, and it smelled delicious.

"Civet de lapin!" Mr. Boncoeur exclaimed, inhaling the aroma. "The stew what I like best is the rabbit stew!"

Rabbit stew. Never had it, never wanted to, but suddenly I was hungry enough to chew my own knuckles. Hey, if I was willing to eat Bambi jerky, why not Easter Bunny stew?

We introduced ourselves over the meal, and the old man explained that he and Louise had come down from Quebec when they were young. At first to work in the shoe mills, and later to run a chain-saw repair service and a woodlot. His real name was Patrice but everybody called him Pete. They had a son who lived not far away, two daughters downstate, and several grandchildren. Louise took a fall a year ago and damaged her spine, which explained the wheelchair.

They wanted to hear my story, too, and when I told them about my journey down the mountain, Pete Boncoeur leapt up, astonished. "No! True word?" he said, tugging on his wispy chin beard. "You come that far in one day? A boy your age?"

"Most of it was downhill."

"Even so. Thirty-five miles, that's a beauty!"

Turns out Concord was fifteen miles farther along the highway. So there was no way I could have made it from Harmony to the hospital in one day as I had planned. The Boncoeurs peppered me with a lot more questions, and even though I don't usually like talking with strangers, I found myself spilling the whole deal. What happened that first night when the lights went out, and then the Superette getting torched, and Reggie Kingman pretending to have a radio connection to the outside world, and the bodies in the trees, and me and the coyotes, and by the time I paused to catch a breath, their eyes were bugging out.

"Louise, *ma chère*, did you hear? Coyotes! Smart you did that, Charlie Cobb, throw him that jerky!"

107

"I guess."

"This a brave thing you do for your mama."

"She's gonna kill me when I get back."

"Ha! Maybe not. So, what next? You find the hospital and get this medicine, then what? Snowshoe back home? All the way up *la montagne*?"

"That's my plan. I know it'll take longer going up than it did coming down, but I'm a good hiker."

The old couple exchanged a secret smile, like they thought I was crazy but were too polite to say so.

It was warm and cozy next to the stove. Soon as I closed my eyes I dove into sleep like an airplane losing power. In my dreams coyotes tried to burn me with their yellow eyes, and I was skiing hard, trying to catch up with my father, but I never did, because he kept vanishing over the horizon like a sun that never quite set.

Worried dreams, anxious dreams.

I woke up very early the next morning to the smell of frying bacon and the sound of Mrs. Boncoeur singing as she prepared breakfast. Something in French that I couldn't understand, except that it was a happy song, a morning kind of song. Her husband was trying to help her cook, and she kept shooing him away, like it was a game they'd been playing all their lives.

It was amazing how well she got around that little kitchen, spinning her wheelchair from the gas range to the insulated coolers to the woodstove. Pouring just-perked coffee into big mugs,

adding evaporated milk and sugar. Making a ton
of home fries and onions in an iron skillet, and
cracking eggs into another pan with steady, clever
hands. Oh yeah, and frying up thin pancakes
dusted with cinnamon and drenched in warm
maple syrup.

Crêpes, she called them. Quebec style. My mom
was a really excellent cook, but I never in my life
tasted anything so good as breakfast from Mrs.
Boncoeur's kitchen.

"Mange pour la vie, mon cher! Eat for life! Eat
enough to get where you going and back."

I stuffed my face until I was full to bursting.
Probably consumed enough calories to circum-
navigate the world. Between that and the coffee—
Mrs. Boncoeur called it *café au lait*—I was roaring
to go. Mom wouldn't allow me to drink full-strength
caffeinated coffee—not until I was fifteen, she
said—and I could see why: it made me feel like a
rocket ready to blast off.

Before I got back on my skis, I restacked the
woodpile and carried as much kindling and firewood inside the house as would fit. The Boncoeurs
kept thanking me—*merci, merci*—and I kept saying
it was nothing, and really it wasn't any big deal, but
they insisted that they wanted to repay the favor.

How they intended to do that was far from clear.
Probably just being polite.

Mrs. Boncoeur waved good-bye from the window, but her husband followed me out into the
yard and made me promise to stop and see them
on the way home.

"You help us, we help you," he said, squeezing my hands through the mittens. "Stop by with us, we help you on your way. Promise you? Cross-your-heart promise?"

I promised. Thinking, *What can a couple of old geezers do for me that I can't do for myself, much as they might want to help?*

Little did I know.

23
BEGGARS NOT WELCOME

Things started going wrong about a mile down the road. For one thing the weather had changed and the temperature was dropping by the minute. The wind mask helped, but the ice-cold air made it hard to breathe. And then when I did get warmed up and started making a little progress, the wind suddenly changed direction and increased velocity. Blowing right in my face and slowing me to a crawl.

I swear, if I hadn't kept fighting for every stride, the wind would have been pushing me backward. What did Mr. Mangano call it? The polar vortex? Believe me, after several hours of fighting the freezing wind, I had juicier names for it.

Took me most of the day to cover those fifteen miles to Concord. When I finally made it to that cloverleaf, nothing looked like I remembered. Partly that's because there were high banks of ice-covered snow blocking the view from the highway level—it was like slogging through a wind tunnel—and partly because when I did get a glimpse of the city, the buildings somehow looked wrong.

Took me a while to figure out why: a lot of them were scorched. Not burned to the ground, but blackened by interior fires, leaving behind sooty stains that made the empty windows look like raccoon eyes.

The city looked half-dead.

Only thing that stopped me from crying was knowing that tears would make my eyeballs freeze solid. First thing was to get down off the highway and out of the wind. Maybe find someplace to warm up and ask directions to the hospital.

Rather than loop around the exit ramp—must have been a mile—I took off the skis, put them over my shoulder, and clambered down the embankment. Had to slide partway on my butt, but managed to get to city street level without breaking a leg or ankle.

Out of the wind, the stink of the fire was even stronger. There were big lumps everywhere along the streets—must have been hundreds of vehicles buried under the snow and ice. But what I noticed most was what wasn't there.

Where was everybody?

Maybe there was a clue across the street, where a good-sized convenience store had been boarded up with sheets of plywood. Spray-painted on the plywood, in bright orange letters three feet high:

LOOTERS WILL BE SHOT ON SIGHT

Below that someone had added a skull and crossbones, and the warning:

OWNER SHOOTS FIRST, GOD ASKS QUESTIONS LATER

I wondered if there might be a map of the city in the store, something looters wouldn't bother stealing, but decided it wasn't worth the risk of finding out. I'd just have to locate the hospital on my own.

I picked a direction and started walking, skis over my shoulder. No way to ski down these lumpy streets anyhow. And it was a relief not to be stretching my legs quite so much.

A couple blocks later I passed a Laundromat. The plate-glass windows were missing and snow had drifted deep inside, covering most of the washers and dryers. Sprayed on the wall: *24-HOUR CURFEW* and *BEGGARS NOT WELCOME* and *IF YUR FROM AWAY GO AWAY.*

Friendly place.

A few more blocks and I came upon a modern motel complex set back from the street. I smelled kerosene burning, and firewood, and the snow had melted from parts of the roof, so it had to be warm inside, or at least above freezing. There was a motel sign in the empty parking lot, covered up with a blue tarp, and a single word sprayed on the tarp, in big drippy letters: *FULL.*

I set my sights on the motel office, but as I attempted to cross the parking lot, two men slid out from behind a snowbank. Or rather, a man and a boy about my age.

The man had a Remington pump shotgun, and the boy hefted an ax.

"Turn around while you got the chance," the man said. "Can't you read? We're full up. No room at the inn."

"I'm not looking for a place to stay. All I need, directions to the hospital."

"This isn't the chamber of commerce," the man said. "Be on your way."

"Dad," said the boy plaintively.

The man glanced at him, shrugged. "Okay. Fine. Hospital is half a mile over that way, but it won't do you any good. It's closed. Empty. Nobody home."

Closed, empty. That hit me like a punch to the gut. Had I come all this way for nothing? I needed to see it with my own eyes.

As I started to leave the boy called out, "Where are you from?"

I turned back to face him. "Harmony."

"Never heard of it."

"Up in the mountains. Small town."

"I know it," the man said, sounding slightly less suspicious. "What do you really want?"

"Medicine for my mother."

"Looters took everything," the man said, shaking his head. "Stripped the hospital clean. I doubt there's an aspirin left."

"There has to be," I said. "There just has to."

The boy said, "Dad? Maybe ask Mom? She's a nurse," he added with pride. "Used to work at the hospital, before it closed."

"Shut it," the man said, glaring at the boy and at me. Then he relented. "Go on. See what she says."

When I tried to follow, the man raised the barrel of the shotgun and said, "Harmony boy, you stay right there. If my wife has something to say, she'll let us know."

We waited in the frozen parking lot for five minutes, or maybe it was a thousand years, with him not quite pointing the shotgun at me, and me not quite having the courage to run away.

The fact is, I was too scared to move. Not of the shotgun—he wouldn't shoot me, I was pretty sure of that—but of what his wife, the nurse, might have to say.

24
ANYWHERE BUT THERE

"Nobody knew what to do," the boy's mother explained.

Her name was Ida Mae Rand. The man with the shotgun was her husband, Joel—he managed the motel—and her son was JJ, for Joel, Jr. She was wearing an oversized skimobile suit and about three layers on top of that, including a fur-lined hat that covered about half of her chubby, freckled face.

Mrs. Rand's nose was running, and instinct made me back up. Couldn't afford to get sick. She smiled—she knew why I'd backed away and didn't blame me. Her bloodshot blue eyes were sad, as if she was carrying the weight of the world on her shoulders, and I guess she was, once I heard her story.

"We had ninety-four patients in the hospital as of New Year's Eve. That's light—believe it or not,

116

quite a few patients asked to be discharged so they could celebrate with families at home. The big show in the sky, you know? God's fireworks. Anyhow, we lost ten in the first forty-eight hours after the power went out. All of the pumps and monitors failed, so it was difficult and sometimes impossible to medicate correctly, or keep them warm. No heat, of course. Backup generator system didn't work. At the time we kept assuming they'd fix it, but of course they couldn't. No one could. And so patients started dying."

Mrs. Rand gave a deep, shuddering sigh and wiped her nose on the back of her mitten.

"Basically the hospital froze, okay? Nothing we could do. Relatives and friends started to trickle in, at least those who lived nearby, and collected their loved ones. Heaven knows how some of them got home. One had a sled, I know that, an American Flyer. Well, the weaker patients began to expire from exposure—we just couldn't keep their body temps up. After five days the hospital was like a walk-in freezer. We had to get the remaining patients someplace warm or they would surely perish. Staff who could take them into their own homes did so. I got the last five, brought 'em to the motel, did the best we could. Three have survived, and one is feeling so good he's been helping Joel with the heating system they jury-rigged."

"Gravity feed, like a big kerosene camp stove," her husband chimed in proudly. "We've got enough fuel oil for another month or so, so we're praying for an early spring."

He was no longer pointing the shotgun at me, but he wasn't putting it away, either.

Mrs. Rand continued. "A week or so after we abandoned the facility, this gang shows up. I say *gang* because some of them were wearing biker colors. Must have been twenty men, well armed. Some towing big toboggans to carry what they looted. They stripped the place clean. Medical supplies, furniture, sheets and towels and blankets. They took it all, including the pharmacy. I know because I went back there looking for medication for one of my patients. Nothing. Bare shelves."

"Told you," her husband said. "Those boys didn't leave so much as an aspirin. Stole everything useful and towed it back to Manchester, or wherever they came from."

"There was nobody to stop them," Mrs. Rand said. "We hadn't organized ourselves yet, and most of the police had left, you know, to care for their own families as best they could. State police, local police, first responders, gone. Can't blame them. Everybody in the same boat, worried about their loved ones freezing to death. Maybe it wasn't so bad out in the north country, a lot of homes heat with wood pellets and such, or have backup woodstoves. But here in the city it's a different story. Mostly oil heating systems, modern burners and thermostats. Electricity required. So nothing works."

She sighed and shook her head, as if ashamed. "I want an early spring like everybody else. But I dread it, too, because it won't be until the weather warms that we know how many people died of exposure. Froze to death in their own homes. More than a few, I imagine."

"Right now we're not thinking about it," her husband said firmly. "Deal with today, let tomorrow take care of itself."

But it was obvious his wife was thinking about it even if he wasn't. And probably that's why she dragged herself out into the frozen parking lot, to talk to a stranger in need.

"How about drugstores?" I asked.

"Sold out or looted. Shelves empty."

"There must be something," I said, my voice cracking.

"Might be," Mrs. Rand said warily. "What exactly is the medication your mother requires?"

I fumbled around in my backpack and showed her an empty pill bottle. She squinted at it and nodded to herself.

"Don't get your hopes up," she said. "But I know a place might have a stock of that drug, or the generic equivalent."

Then she told me where the medicine might be located.

Oh no, was my first thought, *anywhere but there.*

25
THE DOOR AT THE END OF THE HALL

Gronk had a dumb joke he'd try out on anyone who would listen.

How many crazy people in New Hampshire? Enough to fill a loony bin, and one left over—you!

What he didn't mention was that his grandmother had died at the state mental asylum. I don't know exactly what was wrong with her, but it was bad enough so his family couldn't take care of her. Maybe that's why he made jokes about the loony bin, because it hit so close to home.

Unlike Gronk, I'd never known anyone with serious mental illness. So I didn't have any excuse for why the idea of a mental hospital gave me the creeps. But it did. I mean it's not like Freddy Krueger was in there, or Slender Man or Jigsaw. I'm not that stupid. And it's not like the failure of electricity hadn't made everyone at least a little bit crazy—look at Mr. Bragg with his wack ideas, or

King Man with his made-up radio broadcasts. Or me thinking I could ski fifty miles in one day, just because I wanted it to be true.

So if we're all wack, what was the big deal, right?

Mrs. Rand had given me a map, carefully drawn on a scrap of paper. Eleven blocks down the main street, then a right for six more blocks, then look on the left for a red brick building with nine narrow windows facing the street.

"Kind of Gothic," she said.

I didn't know what that meant, except old.

"What do I do when I get there?" I had asked.

"Knock on the door. Ask for Lydia. Tell her I sent you."

On Mrs. Rand's advice I kept to the center of the street, moving at a brisk pace. Slow down, or approach any of the occupied buildings, and you'd likely be challenged by neighborhood patrols. Folks had banded together for heat and mutual protection. Outsiders were not welcome.

"You see a smoking chimney, keep your distance," Mr. Rand had said.

Good advice, as it turned out. With skis and poles slung over my shoulder, I trudged along with a purpose. Men with rifles watched from doorways, or from behind piles of dirty snow, but nobody challenged me, not so long as I kept moving.

I had never felt so all alone, not even when the coyotes were stalking me. It was worse, somehow, to know that fellow humans wanted you gone from their sight.

Following Mrs. Rand's map I came to what looked like a college campus. Kind of pretty, or would have been if the trees hadn't all been cut down, leaving rude, hand-chopped stumps. Firewood, no doubt. Anyhow, all these stately brick buildings with ice-frosted windows glinting in the lowering sun. For the most part they looked abandoned, some with doors standing open and snow drifted inside.

The red brick building with nine windows facing the street was smaller than some of the others, and looked older, with a high-peaked slate roof and a tall brick chimney. Maybe that's what Mrs. Rand meant by *Gothic*. The roof was free of snow, which meant the building was warm inside. I knew for sure it wasn't abandoned because someone was watching me from the center window on the second floor.

A hairless man with a round, moony face and eyes that didn't look right. When I glanced up, he covered most of his face with a curtain. But not his eyes, which seemed to be lit from within, as if by some glowing lamp inside his mind.

It was all I could do not to run away.

Mental illness is an illness, I know that. Nothing to cause this much fear. But me and Gronk must have downloaded too many horror movies, because my hands were shaking as I knocked on the heavy wooden door. And I was almost hoping no one would answer, so I could give up and find my way home. Tell everybody I tried but failed, then wait for the world to fix itself so it wouldn't matter about the medicine.

The door opened a few inches, secured by a thick brass chain.

"Yes?"

"Ida Mae Rand s-s-sent me. I'm looking for L-l-lydia."

The chain slipped off and the door opened.

"Quickly, mustn't let in the cold. Your teeth are chattering."

I stepped inside, holding my skis upright, shedding gobs of snow from my boots.

The woman who answered the door was small and slender and had a plaid wool blanket wrapped over her nurse's uniform like a cape—it wasn't freezing inside, but it wasn't that warm, either. Her silvery white hair was short and tufted, as if she cut it herself. She was as pale as the snow, and obviously wary of strangers, but her eyes were kindly. "I'm Lydia," she said. "How is Ida Mae?"

"Good, I guess."

"You guess?"

"I only met her today. At the motel. She said maybe you could help me."

Lydia looked from me to the skis and back. "You're not from around here."

So I told her where I was from, and how I got there, and why. Words tumbling out.

"Oh my," she said. "That's quite a story." She locked the front door behind us, *clunk,* and said, "You need something hot to drink. That will help with the chattering teeth."

She beckoned, and I followed her down a dark-paneled hallway with high, shadowy ceilings, barely illuminated by the waning daylight. At the end of the hall she paused, raised a key from a chain around her waist, and unlocked a heavy door.

"Don't be afraid," she said before pushing it open. "Some of my residents may say things you find strange, but they won't harm you. Best just to nod and agree."

I nodded like a bobblehead doll as we entered the asylum.

26
BUTS AND BEES AND HONEY TREES

There's a show my mother liked about this rich British family that lives in a castle, except they call it an "abbey." Like rich people will call some humongous mansion on the lake a "cottage." Yeah, right. Anyhow, the characters on the show talk like they have their jaws wired shut, but Mom loved it, and dabbed her eyes with a Kleenex at the sappy parts.

If you've ever seen the show, you may remember it has this big, lovely kitchen with high ceilings. A huge oven takes up most of one wall, and there's a long wooden table the servants sit at when they're finally allowed to eat.

This kitchen was like that, except with mental patients instead of servants. Or residents, as Lydia liked to call them.

My first impression: relief that the man with the moony face and the shining eyes wasn't among

125

them. The ones I did see looked normal enough. They weren't wearing pajamas and bathrobes like in a regular hospital—everybody was dressed in layers, because even with the oven going it was almost cold enough to see your breath.

Okay, to be honest, some of Lydia's residents were a little twitchy, but then I was pretty nervous myself.

"People, this is Charlie Cobb. He has traveled all the way from the north country looking for help."

"He's only a boy boy. Too young to be crazy crazy."

"Tammy, what did we discuss about the use of that word?"

"Crazy is lazy, find a better word, bird. Yadda yadda yadda."

"Thank you, Tammy. Could you heat up some water for tea? I promised young Mr. Cobb a cup of something hot. He's come a very long way on a very cold day."

There were seven residents gathered around the long table, as close to the stove as they could get. A few were playing cards and barely looked up when I entered the kitchen. One appeared to be asleep with his head in his arms. Another was at work on a box of candle stubs, trimming the wicks with a small pair of scissors—she glanced up quickly and looked away without making eye contact.

The only really talkative one was Tammy, a gaunt woman with hair braided tight to her forehead and bunching out around her Red Sox cap. Her mouth was always moving in this strange way, as if she was trying to shape words, and she kept stroking her face with her fingertips. Always moving restlessly. As she waited for a kettle to warm she danced from one foot to the other. "Watch pot never boil," she said, singsonging. "Boil toil, double and trouble. Yadda yadda yadda."

Tammy said *yadda yadda yadda* a lot.

Lydia smiled tolerantly and lowered herself into a wooden chair on the opposite side of the stove, indicating that I do the same. "What did Ida Mae tell you about us?" she asked.

"Not much. She said it was, um, a mental hospital, and that you still had a pharmacy."

"Mmm. Hospital would be too grand a term. More like a refuge. The actual psychiatric facility has been abandoned and most of the patients dispersed elsewhere. Either back to their families or placed with volunteers. The city may look like an armed encampment—and in some ways it is—but there are still plenty of good people out there. I would argue the vast majority. As for this place, it dates to the last century and was most recently a student nurse dormitory. We are, or were, associated with the medical school in Hanover. The students left, needless to say. We needed smaller and warmer quarters, and this old kitchen, as you can see, has an antique stove that will run on kerosene, and some of the rooms have fireplaces that still function. So here we are, making the best of a difficult situation."

Tammy made a noise like a whistling teakettle as she poured water into a pot. "Two for tea, not for me," she said in her singsong voice. "Yadda yadda yadda."

Lydia noticed my unease and said, "Tammy's quirks are the result of tardive dyskinesia. Damage to her nervous system from powerful medication she was given as a child. Mistakenly, as it turned out. But the short version: she can't help it. Trust me when I tell you she has a good head and a better heart."

"Oh," I said, feeling ashamed. "Sorry."

"No need to apologize. As for a pharmacy, when we vacated the main facility, I gathered up all the medical supplies I could find and brought them here in cardboard file boxes. Mostly meds required by the residents—antipsychotics and antidepressants and the like. But long-term residents suffer from a variety of physical ailments, so we have quite a selection. Type 2 diabetes, you said?"

I handed her the empty pill bottle.

"Might be, might not," she said, very casually. "I'll check first thing in the morning."

Seeing my expression, she explained. "If I find what you're looking for, you'll be out that door in ten seconds. Out in the dark and freezing cold in a place that can be very dangerous to strangers, even a young stranger with the face of an angel. I will not have that on my conscience. So. We wait until morning."

"But—"

"No buts. Drink your tea. Honey?"

Tammy sang, "Buts and bees, buts and bees, buts and bees and honey trees. Yadda yadda yadda."

*   *   *

So that's how I ended up spending the night in a mental asylum and playing cards with the residents. I begged Lydia again to check for the medicine right away, and promised to stay the night no matter what, but she insisted on waiting until morning. Finally I gave up. She wasn't that much bigger than me, but she might as well have been made of platinum and steel. Plus she was as stubborn as my own mom would have been in a similar situation. Beg all you want, the answer was no.

Anyhow, playing gin rummy with the residents made me a little uneasy at first, but all in all it was pretty cool. One of the guys, Paul, he was really funny, cracking jokes about now that electricity was gone he no longer had to wear an aluminum foil hat to protect his brain from radio waves. Like he wanted to put me at ease by joking, which reminded me of Gronk, so it worked. This other dude, Edgar, had a lot of trouble focusing on the game—he blinked a lot, like there was something wrong with his eyes—but he explained how his medicine silenced some of his anxiety problems and made him realize he wasn't alone in the world. He said struggling to survive had given them all a sense of purpose, and the understanding that in many ways they were lucky.

"We have Lydia, who saved us and made us a family," Edgar said. "We have this beautiful kitchen, and enough food and medicine to keep us alive and stable. So we count our blessings."

"You and me makes one two three!" Tammy sang, dancing in place and making faces. "Yadda yadda yadda!"

"And we have Tammy, who sings to say, 'Hello, I'm still here and I'm still me.'"

"Yadda yadda yadda!"

"Exactly," he said.

27
INVISIBLE TOYS

I hadn't been so anxious about what morning would bring since the Christmas before my father passed. Me and Becca waking each other before sunrise and then having to wait—hours and hours, or so it seemed—until my parents got up. That's what it was like at the refuge (I started thinking of it that way after the card game) where I slept on a cot in the hall, under a pile of quilts and blankets. Thinking about Mom and how great it would be if I came home with the medicine she needed. I'd be such a hero they might even give me a parade, and King Man would lead the parade and lead the Pledge of Allegiance like he always did, and the whole town would cheer me, and even sour Mr. Bragg would be impressed.

I never did sleep, not really, so I was already awake when Lydia slipped into the hallway, carrying a lantern. It was like watching a star

131

come steadily toward me, glowing warm in the frosty dark.

She placed the lantern on the floor and sat on the end of the cot. "I suppose you were awake all night, worrying," she said. "Sorry about that. Couldn't be helped."

Under the covers I clasped my hands together, over my heart. *Please, please, please.*

"The fact is, Ida Mae knew what she was doing, sending you here. She was aware that one of my residents died soon after we moved, of pulmonary heart failure—he couldn't take the cold, poor man—and that he had type 2 diabetes, among various other ailments."

She placed a jumbo-sized plastic pill bottle in my hands. I gave it a shake. It sounded almost full. "Today is my lucky day," she said. "Old Jim Cronin would be pleased to know that his medication is helping someone else. It's a fitting memorial. But I do worry how you'll get home."

"The same way I came."

She chuckled. "You think I don't know the difference between downhill and uphill?"

"I'll make it, promise."

"It doesn't seem right, letting a boy your age attempt such a dangerous journey on his own."

"Kids my age or younger used to fight in wars."

Lydia sighed. "Some still do. That doesn't make it right, but I can't confine you against your will, even for your own safety, not with your mother's life at stake." She picked up the lantern. "Off you go, then, before I change my mind."

132

The residents had put together a package of food for me, including a still-warm loaf of bread. Tammy had stayed up all night, learning how to bake, and finally got it right. She was so pleased to give it to me that she didn't say anything at all, just grinned from here to tomorrow. Edgar contributed a small jar of peanut butter from his personal stash. Paul didn't have any food to give, so he presented me with a spare deck of cards. "You can play solitaire," he said. "I give you permission to cheat."

"Thanks," I said. "I hope to see you all again sometime."

Paul said, "Not on a professional basis, we hope!" and laughed like a loon. A very funny loon.

I was out by the entrance to the refuge, adjusting my ski bindings and putting on my mittens, when the hairless man in the upstairs window appeared out of nowhere. A great big guy with a moony face and wild shiny eyes and no eyebrows, wearing so many layers of clothes he looked like a ragged planet.

For such a big dude he had a surprisingly high voice. Oddly childish. Almost like he had a little kid inside who did all the talking.

"Want to know a secret?" he asked. "Huh, do you?"

I didn't dare say no.

"Lydia isn't really our nurse, she's one of us!" he hissed. "She's in charge because we gave her the keys!"

"Okay," I said, backing slowly away.

His eyes got bigger and rounder. "Or maybe I'm delusional. Or maybe I'm the man in the moon. Or maybe I'm nobody at all."

"You're not nobody."

He hesitated, as if he wanted to share another secret but didn't quite dare. "You can come to my room if you want," he said. "I have invisible toys."

"Maybe some other time, okay? I have to go home."

"Okay." He headed back inside, then turned and beamed at me. "Don't forget me," he said.

How could I ever?

28
REMEMBER THE INUIT

I found my way back to the highway and climbed the cloverleaf and headed north. Felt like the buildings of the city were watching me with their empty-window eyes. It was cold beyond belief, but lucky for me there was almost no wind so I was able to push and stride like mad for the first couple of miles. Slight incline but that was okay, a good pair of cross-country skis grip the snow and prevent you from sliding backward. Thank you, Gronk.

I wondered what he was thinking. What Mom and Becca and King Man were thinking. What were they doing at exactly that moment? Gronk would be doing chores. Becca, too, because Mom would want to keep her busy. If I knew Mom, she was over being angry at me and was just plain worried. And Becca, well, if anybody understood why I had to do it, Becca did.

Gone for medicine. Be back as soon as I can.

I intended to keep that promise, but a couple of hours of slogging up the highway made it very clear: coming down was the easy part. My plan was to cross-country ski as far as I was able, then hike the rest of the way home, using snowshoes wherever the snow was too deep. I'd have to find places to sleep along the way, preferably where the coyotes couldn't find me.

Figure ten hours of daylight each day. Even if I only averaged a measly two miles an hour, I'd be home in three days. Unless a blizzard shut me down. Then all bets were off.

No blizzards, please. No coyotes. No surprises.

Fifteen miles to the Boncoeurs' house. I did it in one day, going in the other direction. And against the wind, too. When I promised Pete and Louise I'd stop by on the way back, I was thinking of it as a courtesy. No longer. Now it had become a necessity, and as I hauled myself up each yard of snow-packed highway, I dreamed about the warmth of their tidy house, and the smell of Mrs. Boncoeur's cooking, and how odd and wonderful it was that they felt like old friends, even though we'd only recently met.

The sun was about halfway up the sky when my knees and arms began to tremble with exhaustion. Gripping the poles became difficult. No idea how far I'd come, but for sure there was still a long way to go. So I had to buck up and ski through the weakness. I had to keep going.

Plant your poles. Stride. *Push with your legs, pull with your poles.* Stride, stride.

Keep moving, whatever it takes.

I knew what I was supposed to do, but somehow it wasn't working. My legs were so weak they were making me dizzy. Was this how Mom felt when she was having one of her spells?

Take a break, Charlie. Eat something. Drink something, too.

Not sure how it happened, but I ended up on my butt, with the skis tangled under me. It was all I could do to peel off my mittens and punch the binding release with my thumb, and get loose without spraining my ankles.

For a couple of minutes there, what I really wanted was to lie down in the snow and take a little nap. Bad idea.

You're not thinking clearly, Charlie. Don't forget to breathe.

I rolled over, up on my knees, and forced myself to deeply inhale the frigid air. Hurt my lungs but that was okay because it helped to clear my head. I fumbled around, retrieved the package of food provided by my friends at the refuge, intending to finish the loaf of bread.

Frozen solid.

What to do? What was it Mom always said in her teacher voice?

Study. Think. Solve.

I zipped open my parka, tucked the bread inside, zipped it back up. Warmth from my body would thaw the bread out, eventually. Should have thought of that earlier, before it froze.

Next stop, peanut butter. The jar was icy to the touch, and the peanut butter was really thick, but not so thick I couldn't scoop it out and get it into my mouth.

Not so much you choke on it, son. Just a taste.

I worked my tongue against the clot of peanut butter sticking to the roof of my mouth. Breathing heavily through my nose. Which hurt, but so what? Humans need calories. Calories help keep us warm. Remember the Inuit.

I could almost hear Mr. Mangano telling us how Inuit seal hunters ate lots of raw blubber because it helped keep them warm and strong. And if the human body falls below a certain temperature, you go into shock.

I wasn't sure what shock was, except that it was bad. Was I in shock? Was that why I felt so weak?

I sucked snow from my mittens, letting it melt in my mouth. Then did it again and again. Slowly the peanut butter dissolved and warmed my throat going down. And then it warmed my stomach, and the dizziness passed, and I was able to stand without wobbling.

Get a grip! I urged myself. *Remember you can't do it all in one day. Today the goal was fifteen miles and you're at least halfway there. Pay attention. Keep your eyes peeled for that embankment shielding their house from the highway. You don't want to pass it by.*

I strapped the poles to the skis and hefted them over my shoulder. I intended to hike for the next few miles, give my legs a rest, sort of, because walking uses different muscles. The snowpack was dense along that stretch of highway, and I was able to trudge along pretty good. No problem breaking through, and therefore no need for snowshoes, which required at least as much effort as cross-country skis.

For a while I tried pretending I was a soldier marching into battle. Left right, left right. I remembered from one of my class projects that in the Civil War, soldiers carried at least sixty pounds and sometimes covered thirty miles a day on foot. And sometimes barefoot! At least I had really good insulated boots, and I wasn't toting anything like sixty pounds. Ten pounds tops, not counting the skis.

Left right, left right. Enemy in sight, sir! March to the sound of gunfire! Left right! Left right!

The last time we all went someplace together as a family was the weekend before Dad got killed. We drove over to Gorham and hiked Mount Crescent, along this beautifully groomed trail. Two miles up to the summit. Gorgeous winter day. Sun so bright off the snow that we had to put on sunscreen and wear dark goggles. Dad looked really cool in his, like he could have been climbing Everest. The skier's tan made his teeth look really white. I remember Mom laughing a lot and pointing out the birds. Becca just beaming, because she loved it when we did outdoors stuff together.

I felt so lucky that day, to be part of such a great family.

You still are. Don't forget it, never forget.

March, soldier, march! Left right, left right! Marching home, marching home.

March for your sister, march for your mom, keep on marching or you'll be a bum!

Left! Right! Left! Right!

After an hour or so I checked the bread and it was soft enough to eat. Peanut butter on bread was an improvement on just plain peanut butter, and it seemed to give me strength and lift my spirits.

Left right. Left right. And keep your eyes peeled for that embankment, because it hides the Boncoeur place and you don't want to miss it or you'll be sleeping out in the cold. Food for bears. Coyote bait.

As it turned out there was no way to miss it because they had left me a sign by the side of the highway. An actual spray-painted sign with my name on it and an arrow pointing at their house.

This way Charlie Cobb

29
BETTER THAN CHRISTMAS

It took me hours to warm up, even with the wood-stove blazing and the house as cozy as could be. Mrs. Boncoeur encouraged me to slurp down about a gallon of hot, salty chicken broth, and gradually I stopped shivering and began to feel like my normal self.

The elderly couple waited patiently to hear about my adventure, but Pete finally couldn't contain himself any longer.

"So?" he asked. "Your quest? Did you meet with success?"

My grin was my answer, and they both seemed to be as happy about it as I was, which was nice. That got me rolling and I ended up describing all the stuff that happened since I left their house. How tough the going was those last fifteen miles with the wind in my face, and the eerie, half-burned city on guard against gangs and looters, and Mrs. Rand

sending me to the asylum, and the friends I made
there, and Lydia giving me enough medication to
last Mom until spring, and the man in the moon
saying don't forget.

When I was done, Mrs. Boncoeur beckoned me
to her wheelchair, threw her arms around me, and
kissed my wind-chapped forehead. "*Très bon*, very
good," she said. "A boy came down the mountain,
a man goes back up."

"What she say, double that!" Pete said.

"You've been busy," Mrs. Boncoeur said, warming my hands in hers. "We've been busy, too.
Arrangements have been made, *mon cher*! Tomorrow you go home in style!"

Arrangements have been made? Go home in
style? What was she talking about? The old couple
was super nice and everything, but what could
they possibly do to help, beyond providing a hot
meal and a warm place to sleep?

Pete Boncoeur, beaming with pride, explained
exactly what had been arranged for my benefit.
And if I hadn't already been sitting down I'd have
fallen right to the floor.

Shortly after dawn I hugged Mrs. Boncoeur good-
bye and followed Pete out into the front yard, not
far from the woodpile that had almost killed him.
It was intensely cold, but there was almost no wind,
and our frosty breath hung in the air like smoke.

The old man unzipped his parka pocket and
withdrew a bright orange flare gun. A gift from
their son, Renny, who lived about three miles away,

just over the horizon. Who needs smoke signals to communicate if you have a flare gun?

"You ready, Charlie? Won't take long, once he sees the flare."

"I'm ready."

Pete aimed at the top of the sky, where the stars were just beginning to fade, and pulled the trigger. With a whoosh the flare streaked upward, bursting into a bright, sizzling flame, and then very slowly descended under its own little parachute.

We heard them coming long before we could see them. The excited, high-pitched yipping of running dogs. Pete squeezed my arm and said, "This is the beauty part," and right on cue the sled dogs burst through an opening in the trees, running so hard and fast their blurred feet didn't seem to touch the snow.

Crouched on the sled, urging on the blue-eyed dogs and grinning like he loved it, was a young version of Pete Boncoeur. Same jutting chin beard, but the younger beard was black, and the man who leapt from the sled was slightly taller and way more nimble than the old man.

"Charlie Cobb, meet our son, Renny Boncoeur," Pete said with unmistakable pride. "He and his team of huskies, they win the thirty-mile sprint last year at Bretton Woods. Lots of other races, too."

Renny clapped his leather mittens together, more or less silencing the eager dogs. He grinned at me and said, "You're not going to need those skis today. Not if me and the dogs have anything to say about it."

I explained that the skis belonged to my friend Gronk and that I had promised to return them.

"Oh yeah? Okay then!" Renny declared. "No problem. We'll make room."

He tied the skis and poles and my backpack to the sled, then strode into the house to greet his mother, who had been waving from the window.

He returned a few minutes later with a thermos of coffee and showed me where to sit in the racing sled and how to brace myself.

"Ever ride a dogsled, young man?"

"No, sir."

"Ha! Better than flying. We'll do all the work. You pull down your ski mask, sit back, and enjoy the ride. Bye-bye, Papa! Bye, Mama. I'll be home for dinner!"

Renny gave a shout and the dogs strained forward, tightening the harness. He ran behind to get the sled going and then we were on our way, gathering speed as the dogs quickly got into rhythm. Tails up like furry exclamation points, their beautiful thick coats bristling in the cold.

The amazing thing, they all panted at the same time in the same way, ten red tongues wagging together, first one side of their mouths, then the other, like the tick-tock on a cuckoo clock. I glanced back and saw Renny's eyes so big they nearly filled his goggles. He was supposed to be a professional racer, but he seemed to be just as excited about the ride as me.

The sled was equipped with brakes, but I don't think he ever used them. I'd only ever seen a dogsled race on TV and had no idea what it would feel like, sitting that low to the ground and going that fast.

It felt jet-propelled, that's how it felt. Or maybe dog-propelled was more like it. For sure it seemed faster than most snowmobile rides, with the ground blurring by only inches from my face. Careening through the woods on narrow trails that hadn't been groomed since the power failed. Crossing snow-blasted meadows and frozen ponds and mountain passages, through sunlight and shadow, with Renny Boncoeur clinging to the sled and yipping like his huskies, shouting, "Gee to the swing dog! Haw to the swing dog! Pull for the lead dog! Hi! Hi! Hi! On Aby! On Aleu! On Ada and Bullet and Cricket! On Hotfoot! On Juno! On Miki and Suka and Stash! On, you huskies, on!"

It was a song of speed and endurance, of strength and skill. A song of friendship, passed from parents to son. A song that filled me with real joy for the first time since my father had passed. And why not? I had the medicine in my pocket—mission accomplished—and a fast ride home that was a dream come true. Except I never could have dreamed it! I'd thought it would take me days and days to fight my way back up the mountain, trudging on snowshoes and boots, but with the help of some good people and a team of amazing dogs, I'd be sleeping in my own bed tonight.

It was better than Christmas, better than candy, better than anything I could have imagined.

Oh, and how the dogs loved it! You could feel the joy in them, too, the harnesses singing with their strength. The sled going airborne as we hit bumps in the trail. The sled runners zinging over the ice and through the crusted snow. The dogs yip-yipping with the ferocious fun of running together as a pack, pulling as one.

They ran twenty miles, most of it uphill, in one hour and thirty-four minutes, before Renny called a halt. He had an old windup wristwatch, so he knew. He unhooked the dogs from their tug leashes so they could chomp on snow and then use the ground.

"Not bad," he said, nodding with satisfaction. "At this rate we'll get you home by noon."

"Amazing" was all I could say, my heart still hammering.

He poured a small cup from the thermos and handed it to me. "Mama said you like her *café au lait*. Good stuff. Caffeine to wake you, milk for your bones, sugar for energy. Drink up!"

Unlike his parents, Renny didn't have a French accent. He sounded pure New Hampshire, and it turned out that when he wasn't training and tending to his dogs he was working for the state, surveying land and highways. But sled racing was his passion.

"When my parents told me what you did for them, and about your mission, I thought, *How perfect.* Because these dogs come from a grand tradition of delivering medical supplies."

His dark eyes gleamed bright as he talked enthusiastically about the husky breed. How they were brought to Alaska from Siberia during the gold rush. How they became really famous when a deadly epidemic hit Nome, and the only way to get serum to save the people was by dogsled.

"They called it the Race of Mercy. Six hundred and seventy-four miles from Nenana to Nome, over the most dangerous terrain on the planet. A hundred and fifty sled dogs made the relay in five days! Over rough ice, through arctic blizzards! Nothing stopped them. Now that was a beauty, as Papa would say. The world held its breath until the people of Nome were saved. The lead dog, Balto, it made him so famous he has a statue in Central Park! So you see, our little sprint today, it's a piece of cake."

"Not to me."

"*Ce n'est rien*, as Mama likes to say. It's nothing." Renny put away the thermos and hooked the team back up to leashes, praising each dog as he did so. "Ready?"

"Yes, please."

Moments later we resumed our journey.

We flew up the trail and across the snowy fields, mile after mile, into the north country, as my new friend sang to his beloved huskies: "Gee to the swing dog! Haw to the swing dog! Pull for the lead dog! Hi! Hi! Hi! On Aby! On Aleu! On Ada and Bullet and Cricket! On Hotfoot! On Juno! On Miki and Suka and Stash! On, you huskies, on!"

It wasn't until the Harmony church steeple poked above the tree line that I thought about what might happen if Webster Bragg and his boys happened to see a team of splendid sled dogs racing into the village.

I wasn't worried that he'd shoot them—no one could be that mean—I was worried that he'd steal them.

As it turned out, Bragg did want to steal something, but it wasn't the dogs.

30
MIGHT, NOT RIGHT

I insisted on skiing the last few miles by myself. It seemed safer that way. I hope Renny didn't think I was trying to hog all the glory, but I really was worried about his sled and dogs, and relieved when they sprinted out of sight and the wild yips gradually faded in the freezing air.

As it turned out I should have been more worried about myself.

My head was full of getting home. Everyone would be surprised to see me back so soon. I'd only been gone a few days so they'd probably assume I'd given up and turned around and the mission failed. What a cool surprise it would be when I handed Mom the bottle! And I couldn't wait to tell Gronk about all of my adventures, especially the wild ride on the sled.

Our house was in sight, smoke curling from the chimney—*I was almost there!*—when men in winter camo and white ski masks stepped out of the woods, raised their AR-15s, and ordered me to halt.

"Drop your poles, son," said Bragg, emerging from behind them and looking very pleased with himself. "This won't take a moment. Everybody has to submit to a search before entering the free state of Liberty."

"The what?"

"Sad to say, America as we knew it no longer exists, so I have taken the next logical step and established a new state. A free state, beholden to no one but us. We call it Liberty, and we are ruled by a single leader. That would be me."

"So you're the king now?"

He laughed, *heh-heh-heh*, and shook his head. "Better than the poor fool you've got at the moment. Leaders lead, son. They seize opportunity when it presents itself. All Reggie Kingman ever seized was another donut. Now please lower your pack to the ground and unzip it, so we can conduct our search. I warn you, contraband will be confiscated, no exceptions."

When I tried to resist, his boys picked me up by the arms and jerked me out of my skis. Never said a word, but they seemed to enjoy it.

"Set him down gently," Bragg ordered. "Save yourself some time, son. Tell us where you hid it."

"Hid what?"

He smiled at me, but his strange pale eyes weren't even slightly friendly. "Heard about your little escapade. The whole town knows, thanks to your friend, who told your sister, who told everyone in town. She thinks you're a hero for trying. And maybe she's right. Are you a hero, son?"

"I'm not your son."

"The point is, did you succeed?"

"No," I told him. "The hospital was looted."

"Is that right? Lot of that going around. Which is another argument for strong leadership."

"Let me go! You have no right!"

That made him smile even more. "This is about might, Charlie, not right. Too much emphasis on individual rights is what ruined this country in the first place! It obscured the fact that in nature only the strongest survive. Encourage the weak and you dilute the race."

"I don't know what you're talking about and I don't care. Let me go!"

"Caucasians are the only pure race, like white is the only pure color," Bragg said, going into lecture mode. "Mix with the darker bloods and we lose our natural superiority. That's not going to happen in Liberty. No way. We're white and we'll stay that way. And to do that we have to control our borders."

"Nothing in his backpack," one of his boys said, scattering my stuff on the snow.

"No, he'd keep it close," Bragg said craftily. "Hold him still."

They seized me by the wrists and ankles, pinning me in place.

"Sorry about this, son. Things would go easier if you just obeyed orders."

Bragg grinned that coyote grin of his as he unzipped my parka. He rooted around the inside pockets, and then with a grunt of satisfaction shook the extra-large pill bottle in my face.

"Consider these confiscated," he said. "If your mother needs medication she can ask me pretty please. From now on everything goes through me. Fuel, firewood, food, medication. Everything. I'll decide who gets what. Understood?"

"No!"

"I hope you will in time. I really do. We're going to need men like you in this brave new world of ours."

"Give those back, they're mine!"

He snorted in disbelief. "Really? You took them from someone else. I took them from you. That makes them mine, to do with as I see fit. We'll confiscate those skis, too. See if we can keep you a little closer to home, for your own protection."

"Those belong to Gronk!"

"Not anymore. Haven't you been listening? Everything belongs to the free state of Liberty, and therefore to me. It's difficult for you to grasp, perhaps, but eventually you'll come to understand that my way is the best way."

"Never!"

He shook his head, pretending to be sorrowful. "Never say never, Charlie. Not if you want your mother to get her pills. Now get out of here, son. Go home and explain the situation. Tell your mother, tell your friends. Tell Kingman. Tell him if he doesn't like the way I'm doing things he can come out to the compound and we'll discuss it, man to man. Or man to donut, if that's what it takes."

Bragg laughed that terrible laugh, and then he and his boys slipped into the woods and were gone.

31
BECCA RISES

This is embarrassing, but when my mom and Becca raced out of the house to greet me with cries of joy and hug me till it hurt, I started weeping. Partly it was the look on their faces: worry and love all mixed up together. But mostly it was Bragg. It felt like he'd reached into my head and flipped a switch and changed everything. The adventure down the mountain, the risks taken, the people who helped me along the way—none of it counted.

He'd stolen more than the pills from me.

Becca said, "I knew you'd make it, Charlie! Everybody said it was too far, but I knew if anyone could do it, you could!"

I decided right then and there not to point out that if she and Gronk had kept my secret, that rotten crud Webster Bragg wouldn't have had a clue. Because they couldn't have known what he would do, and besides, only a jerk would complain when his friends brag about him and think he's brave and stuff. Even when he's not. Even when he's failed.

Mom patted my face dry with her sleeve and kissed me on the forehead. "Your brother must be tired," she said to Becca. "Let's get him inside and let him rest."

I figured the first thing she'd do when she got the chance was read me the riot act, how I'd broken her rule about not skiing, but she never mentioned it. Something had changed, like maybe she'd realized I wasn't a little kid anymore, and had to do things on my own sometimes, even if I failed.

And boy did I blow it this time. I was right to worry about Bragg and his boys, should have found a way to avoid them on the trip back. Circled around somehow. But I was in such a hurry to get home, wanting to be the big hero, that I walked right into his trap. And I was going to have to explain to my mother and my sister that it was all for nothing. I might as well have never tried. Except it was worse, because now we'd have to go begging to Webster Bragg.

I wanted to confess everything, no excuses, but first I needed to calm down so I didn't start weeping again. Some hero, right?

Get a grip. Face the music. Admit I screwed up. The first thing I noticed when we entered the house was what a great job Becca had been doing with the firewood. She had restacked everything neat as a pin, and the stove was the perfect temperature, warm enough to radiate heat but not so hot as to lose it all up the chimney and burn more wood than necessary. Perfect. And totally typical Becca.

I wished she wasn't sitting there beaming at me. That would stop when she heard how I messed up.

Mom handed me a mug of hot cocoa and took a seat opposite me. She, too, was beaming.

This was going to be awful.

"Before you say a word," Mom said, raising a hand, palm out, "your sister and I discussed this. You running off without informing us. And she persuaded me to see how it might look through your eyes. That you wanted to do the right thing, even if it meant risking your life. That you were doing it as much for her as for me."

My jaw dropped. How did Becca get that from a ten-word note? *Gone for medicine. Be back as soon as I can.* That's all I wrote. Of course she talked to Gronk, who filled her in on the details, but still. *Smarter than your average chipmunk.* My father used to tease her by saying that, when she'd done something clever or smart or way ahead of her age. She loved it because she loved chipmunks, and Dad knew that, of course.

"You made it back unharmed. That's all that matters," Mom said. She cleared her throat. "But I do feel it is my duty to impose some sort of punishment."

Here it comes, I thought.

"Therefore you will not watch TV, or play with

your Xbox, or communicate by cell phone for the next twenty-four hours."

She and Becca looked at each other and then burst into giggles. They waited for me to join in, but I just couldn't.

Instead I burst out: "I got the medicine, but Mr. Bragg stole it before I could get home! And Gronk's skis, too!"

It was terrible, seeing the laughter die, and the happiness instantly melt away.

Mom took a deep breath. "He did what? Charlie, start from the beginning."

And so I did. I described how me and Gronk planned it, and he gave me his super-duper sleeping bag and his best skis, and all that venison jerky. How I evaded Bragg and his boys on my way out of town. How far I got that first day, after passing the plane wreck and escaping from the coyotes, and helping the old man out from under his woodpile. I told them everything, the half-burned city, the not-welcome motel, the looted hospital, and Lydia's refuge for mentally ill people who had nowhere else to go. I described the fantastic dogsled ride, which should have been exciting, but my heart wasn't in it, because when I got to the end Bragg was still there, stealing the medicine and Gronk's skis.

When I was done my mother's face looked like it had been chiseled in pale stone, and Becca's eyes were burning with a fierceness that kind of scared me.

"He said what, exactly?"

"Um, that if you needed medicine you'd have to go ask him pretty please."

Becca rose from her seat. Her hands were fisted at her sides. I couldn't quite see the steam coming from her ears, but it had to be there.

"I'm calling a town meeting," she announced, and marched to the door.

Mom said, "Becca, wait. Let's think about this."

"No, Mom. It can't wait."

Out the door she went, no hat or coat or mittens. A few minutes later the church bell began to ring.

32
KING MAN MAKES A PROMISE

Mom was pretty shocked, not only by what Bragg had done but by Becca's act of defiance. She sat there stunned as the church bell rang the call to meeting, and then her face cleared and she said, "Your sister is right. This needs to be done."

We left the house and followed the crowd to the town hall. Not everybody in Harmony showed up, but many did. And most of them seemed to have the wrong idea.

They thought we were gathering to celebrate.

Mrs. Adler hailed me as we entered the hall. "Charlie! That was fast! We're all so proud of you. Congratulations!"

I wanted the Earth to open up and swallow me. It's bad enough to be a failure, but having people think you're a hero when you're not, that's way worse.

159

Reggie Kingman hurried in, smiling and clapping his hands. The moment he saw my expression, his smile froze. I was getting a lot of that. Grins of celebration turning to puzzlement. Gronk ambled in with his parents, ready to party, spoke with Becca for a few moments, and then gave me a look so sorrowful it was like a punch to the stomach.

By the time the seats filled, everybody seemed to understand that something was wrong. This wasn't going to be a party. There wasn't anyone to celebrate, certainly not me.

People stirred uncomfortably on the hard wooden seats, waiting for the bad news. When a hush came over the crowd, Reggie Kingman, who had been seeing to the pellet stove, went to the stage and said, "Thank you all for responding. Rebecca Cobb called this meeting. I think we should hear what she has to say."

I've always known Becca was something special. Not just because she's my sister but because she has such a clear way of seeing things. Even when she was really little she looked at the world like it was a puzzle to be solved. So I shouldn't have been surprised that her gentle, husky voice somehow managed to fill the hall.

"Hello, you all know me. I'm the one who was blabbing about my brother, Charlie, and the cool thing he was trying to do, even though it scared me almost to death." After describing what had happened with me and the medicine and Webster Bragg, she said, "This isn't just about my mother's medicine. Or having to beg from that big creep. Because maybe we would, if that's what it took. This is about what happens next, and that's what worries me. Mr. Bragg wants us to do something, that's why he stole those pills. He's picking a fight. And the only reason a bully ever picks a fight is because he thinks he can win."

Becca paused and looked around, as if searching the room for clues. "Why would he think that?" she asked. "Thank you for listening and now I'll sit down."

When she got back to where me and Mom were waiting in the front row, her chin was trembling but her eyes were dry.

Leave it to my sister to be braver than me.

Kingman cleared his throat and said, "Thank you, Rebecca. You've given us a lot to think about."

Someone in the back of the hall shouted, "What's to think about! Arrest those men and be done with it!"

From the sound of it, he wasn't the only one who felt that way.

Kingman held up his hand, and the crowd went quiet. "It's not that simple. I agree with Rebecca. Bragg did this to provoke a reaction. Figures we'll march out to his compound to confront him. Me and whoever else volunteers. He wants us to do that. Why? Maybe he has an ambush in mind."

"So we do nothing, is that it? Rest of us have been contributing firewood and food. Not that weasel Bragg! He even thieved firewood from the elderly, and you haven't done a thing about it!"

Officer Kingman nodded wearily. He'd heard it all before. "Agreed. Sooner or later we'll have to deal with Mr. Bragg. He and his boys are eager for an excuse to engage in violence. That's obvious. But I don't want blood on my hands, not if I can help it."

"You worried about Bragg's blood or your own?"

Kingman looked a bit shocked by that, but responded readily enough. "You want to know if I'm scared of getting shot? Of course I am. Anybody would be. But mostly I'm worried about my deputies. Those of you who've been generous enough to volunteer. I don't want it on my conscience that I walked you into an ambush."

Gronk's dad, Mr. Small, stood up. He looked nervous, but determined to have his say. "I'll admit it, when this first started I didn't take Webster Bragg seriously. Yeah, he blew away an ATM, and yeah, he spouted a lot of wacky, hateful theories about the end of the world and the New World Order and white supremacy and like that. Forgive me, Naomi, but I still didn't take him seriously when we suspected that one of his boys set fire to the Superette." Mr. Small paused to gather his thoughts. "To be honest I figured they were drunk, simple as that. But I underestimated the man. He's determined to make himself king or dictator or whatever, and despite all that racist, paranoid talk, he's intelligent and therefore all the more dangerous. So I'm with Reggie. We need to do something, but we can't go off half-cocked. We need a plan." He started to sit down, then popped back up.

"Anybody has any good ideas in that regard, I'm listening."

An older woman heaved herself to her feet, way in the back. "What about your special radio, Mr. Kingman? Can we request backup? State troopers, National Guard?"

Kingman couldn't bring himself to look directly at her. "Not at this time, Mildred. We're snowbound. On our own. We'll just have to figure it out ourselves. Right now I'm thinking the best way might be to go out there by myself. See if I can persuade Mr. Bragg to return the medicine as a gesture of goodwill."

Mom, alarmed, leapt to her feet. "Reggie? I don't want you going in there alone. Not for my sake. Please?"

He nodded but held to his decision. "Alone is best, given the situation. I'm the one who attended the police academy. I'm the one who has been trained to respond in situations like this. I'm the one who volunteered for this job."

Nobody said it, but everybody was thinking, *And you're the one who's the best pistol shot in the state, or used to be.*

"And what happens when he says no?" Mom demanded.

"Truth?" His hands slipped to his holster. "I don't intend to take no for an answer, once I manage to get inside. I'll leave with your medicine, Emma, or I won't leave at all."

33
IT HAS BEEN AN HONOR

Looking back, we should have foreseen why Webster Bragg did what he did. Why he stole the medicine and encouraged me to tell everybody about it. Not because he wanted my mother to beg, although he might have enjoyed that. Not because he wanted King Man and his volunteer deputies marching out to his compound. No, he was way smarter than that. He assumed that someone would call a meeting to complain about his behavior. And then he'd have all his opponents trapped in an old wooden building. That was his plan all along.

Should have foreseen it, but we didn't. So it came as a big surprise when Bragg's amplified voice started booming from the street.

"CITIZENS OF HARMONY, STAY WHERE YOU ARE. DO NOT RESIST. LAY DOWN YOUR WEAPONS AND SURRENDER."

164

My first thought was, if electricity isn't working, how can he amplify his voice? The answer was simple, as I saw when sneaking a peek out the window. Bragg was some distance away, more or less protected by a lump of ice that had once been a school bus, but he had in his hands an old-fashioned megaphone, like cheerleaders use at football games. Nothing electric about it, just a big cone-shaped thing that must have been three feet long.

"YOU ARE SURROUNDED. OBEY ME IF YOU WANT TO LIVE!"

He wasn't kidding about the surrounded part. He sons were spread out, crouching behind tree trunks. Like their father, they were in full winter camo and heavily armed. They looked oddly bulky until I realized they were wearing battle armor. Armored vests and body shields. Ready for war.

Then Becca grabbed me and dragged me away from the windows.

"Everybody get down. Hug the floor," King Man ordered.

We got down on the floor. I heard someone crying. All I knew for sure, it wasn't me.

"THERE WILL BE NO NEGOTIATION. THE FREE STATE OF LIBERTY HAS TAKEN CONTROL OF THIS TERRITORY. ALL THOSE WHO LIVE WITHIN THESE BORDERS MUST OBEY THE PRIME LEADER. THOSE WHO RESIDE OUTSIDE THESE BORDERS ARE DEEMED TO BE ENEMIES OF LIBERTY AND WILL BE TREATED ACCORDINGLY."

I was hugging the floor, Becca on one side of me, Mom on the other. Becca's voice was even huskier than usual. "This is my fault," she said. "I rang the bell."

"No, sweetie."

"I'm sorry."

"Don't be sorry. This is his doing."

"I should have listened to you."

"It's not your fault, pumpkin."

I had my cheek to the floor but my eyes were wide open. Focused on the windows because I expected them to dissolve in a hail of bullets. But instead of bullets I saw reflections of light. Flickering light.

Flames.

"FIREBOMBS HAVE BEEN IGNITED AND ARE READY TO LAUNCH. YOU HAVE ONLY ONE CHOICE IF YOU WANT TO LIVE. REGGIE KINGMAN MUST BE SURRENDERED UNARMED OR THE HALL WILL BE BURNED TO THE GROUND WITH ALL OF YOU IN IT!"

Mom had a tight grip on me and Becca. She whispered, "When I say run, we're going to run to the back of the hall. We'll find a way out."

That's when I noticed that Reggie Kingman was clinging to the podium. Like he'd fall down if he let go. I could see the fear in his eyes, and that scared me almost as much as the threat of fire. His mouth was working, trying to speak, and finally he managed to say, in a shaky voice, "Everyone stay calm, please. I'll do my duty."

Nobody said a word. Nobody said *Don't do it, don't give yourself up*, because we all knew the consequences, and we were all as terrified as our volunteer police officer.

A lot of folks couldn't bear to watch. They kept their eyes shut or stared at the floor. Some prayed, some cursed. And some of us couldn't look away from Reggie Kingman as his trembling hands fumbled at his holster.

Hands shaking so bad he couldn't unbuckle the thing.

Finally he sat down on a chair to steady himself, took a deep breath, and managed to unfasten his belt and slowly ease it to the floor.

"YOU HAVE ONE MINUTE. GIVE ME KINGMAN OR BURN."

Kingman's eyes widened at that, and he saw me watching him. Or I'm pretty sure he did, because he nodded in my direction and mouthed the word *sorry* before he hauled himself to his feet. Then he seemed to find his courage. He adjusted his policeman's hat and managed to walk from the podium to the front door without trembling or hesitation, at least not very much.

Before leaving he turned to us and said, "Thank you all. It has been an honor."

Then he opened the door and stepped outside.

I wrenched free of Mom and ran to the window just in time to hear the snapping boom of a rifle shot and see King Man fall to the ground like a puppet with his strings cut.

34
LUCK OF THE DRAW

Despite the threat of being firebombed, everybody crowded to the windows and the open doorway to see what was going on. There we were, more than a hundred men, women, and children, staring down Webster Bragg and his little army.

For a moment, the space of a few heartbeats, nothing happened. And then so many things happened all at once that it took me a while to sort it out later.

First thing, Reggie Kingman was lying on the steps of the town hall, hand clutching his side. His dark blue policeman's hat had fallen off and I could see the bald spot on the back of his head. Never noticed that before. His face was gray, his eyes unfocused.

Then Bragg came out from behind his hiding place. The megaphone had been replaced by an AR-15, and he advanced toward the steps where

Kingman had fallen, as if intending to finish him off.

We remained frozen where we were, not daring to move. Bragg's boys, silent as ever, had their rifles aimed at us. The ones holding firebombs looked eager for a reason to throw. It all seemed to be happening in between ticks of a giant clock, as if we were trapped in the gears, unable to change or stop what was about to happen.

Then someone started yelling from way down the street. A figure was running excitedly toward the town hall, into the sights of the guns. Holding one cupped hand out in front of him, the other waving high in the air as he shouted, "It's back! It's back! It's holding!"

Mr. Mangano, our science teacher. He'd left his house without his parka or hat or mittens, and was so focused on whatever it was he had in his hand that he didn't notice what was going on. Bragg moving in for the kill, weird eyes gleaming with the promise of more bloodshed.

When he finally realized what was happening, Mr. Mangano stopped in his tracks. Horrified, he looked from King Man to Bragg and said, "No, no. Don't do it. Everything has changed."

He opened his hands, revealing the compass. "See? When the lights first went out the needle just wandered. No charge at all. Then about a week ago it started swinging wildly, as if looking for a place to settle. I didn't want to raise any false hopes, or frighten anyone with the prospect it might get even worse, which was a distinct possibility, so I didn't say anything." He looked around, from the gun-men to those of us trapped in the town hall, and begged us to understand. "Maybe I should have. Because in the last few hours, those wild swings started to settle down. And here—look!—it's hold-ing! The compass points north!"

I'd like to say we all understood what it meant, that an old Boy Scout compass was working. That magnetism was functioning once again, and what-ever that implied about electrical current. But the only one who got it, other than Mr. Mangano, was my sister, Rebecca. Little Becca, smarter than your average chipmunk, who called out, "Mom? Charlie? Look! It's working!"

Her hands were cupped around the mini flash-light she wore on a lanyard around her neck.

The flashlight was glowing.

Webster Bragg lowered his AR-15 and backed up a step. He was a hater, but he was a smart guy, too, and I think he had some idea of what was about to happen, and what it might mean for men like him. Men who depended on chaos and fear.

We all heard it at the same time. The *rrr-rrr-rrr* of an internal combustion engine trying to start. And then another and another. All around Harmony, automatic generators cranked over as batteries came to life and current began to flow. Spark plugs sparked. Pistons fired. And one by one, our homes began to fill with incandescent light.

Nobody is sure what happened to Webster Bragg that afternoon. One moment he was about to take charge, the next he and his boys slipped away. Headed back to the compound, probably. Maybe to see if their trucks and Hummers would start. They'd need those vehicles to load up their weapons and their gold, and whatever else they'd been hoarding.

Why did Bragg and his family do what they did? Why did they look at the mean side of things instead of the good? Why did they hate so much? Maybe because the world had changed, and then changed again, and it upset their compasses. But that's only my theory, and what do I know?

One thing I did figure out. Who was behind the pair of high headlights approaching Harmony from the south. It was several hours later, in the evening, and Mrs. Adler and Mom were tending to Reggie Kingman. Applying pressure to slow the loss of blood, keeping him warm with blankets heated on the woodstove, and praying he would survive the night.

The high headlights slowly bobbed as they got closer and closer to town. They belonged to a Tucker Terra Sno-Cat, the one with all-rubber treads, adjustable plow, and a heated cabin. My aunt Beth had commandeered it from the National Guard armory and headed north to check on her sister and family.

She wasn't able to visit longer than it took to load Reggie Kingman into the cab, with Mrs. Adler riding along as a nurse. From there it was decided they'd go straight to the Air National Guard base hospital in Portsmouth, fast as that Sno-Cat would go.

Not very fast, so we were worried about that.

Before she left, Aunt Beth—Staff Sergeant Bethany C. Delaney, Air National Guard, 157 Refueling Wing—told us that the president of the United States would address the nation the next morning, as the sun rose over Washington, D.C. "Gonna take 'em a while to get the cable and satellite networks back up and running, so they'll be doing it the old-fashioned way, by radio. Sunrise in D.C. is about twenty minutes after sunrise here, this time of year. So be ready to tune in."

"What frequency?" Mr. Mangano wanted to know.

"All of 'em," said Beth. "As I understand it they'll be saturating the airways, AM, FM, and shortwave."

Mom embraced her. "I was so worried, little sister! Worried you might have been flying. Worried you might have crashed."

"Luck of the draw," Beth said. "I happened to be off duty. Everybody airborne, they went down, near as we can figure. Lots of friends, lots of colleagues. Nobody is sure what happened. All we know is that it appears to be over. There will be planes back in the air by this time tomorrow, count on it! Meantime, don't forget to tune in. Shortly after dawn. Any frequency."

We didn't forget.

35
REMEMBER THIS

Most of us were there before the sun came up, waiting as Mr. Mangano rigged King Man's old crystal radio to the public address system in the old town hall. It only seemed fitting. We had no idea if Mr. Kingman would survive—he had looked so drained of life as they loaded him into the Sno-Cat, and it was such a long journey—but the idea of a radio-wave beacon of hope, that image would live as long as we did.

Mom came along with me and Becca, not because she really felt like it—she was still a little shaky, maybe because almost getting killed messes with your blood sugar—but because she thought we'd want to remember being together on that particular morning.

We still had the problem of what to do about her pills, which would be running out in less than two weeks. But with power back and vehicles running, I was confident we could find a way. Once the roads were clear we could drive wherever necessary. Or borrow a snowmobile. And Aunt Beth could help, if it came to that.

Meantime, Mom decided I was old enough to drink real coffee, and that was cool. She handed me a cup from the big urn in the town hall, heavy with milk and sugar, and said, "As I recall, you prefer *café au lait*. This won't be as good as Mrs. Boncoeur's, but it will have to do."

Very cool.

Not everybody joined us that morning. Some had radios at home, or were so upset by what had happened on the town hall steps that they didn't want to leave their homes, or the comforting warmth that was finally being provided by generators and heating systems. Some may have been ashamed because in their hearts they had agreed with Webster Bragg and his ideas about how we needed to fear everybody who wasn't us.

But the former town moderator, the old dude with the shakes, Mr. Hubert Brown? He was there, sitting up straight with his ancient hands folded in his lap, looking delighted to be alive. Many of those who had stood with King Man came not only to hear the radio broadcast, but also to inquire about the status of our volunteer police officer.

Like I said, we didn't know what happened after the Sno-Cat left because cell phone service had not yet been restored, and landlines were down, and would be for a long time.

Gronk's father said if anybody could survive a wound like that it would be Reggie Kingman, but he didn't sound like he really believed it.

"Bravest thing I ever saw," he said, shaking his head in admiration. "The man was scared to death but willing to take a bullet for us. Don't know what it says in the dictionary, but that's my definition of courage."

Gronk slipped into the seat between me and Becca, grinning like it was his birthday and he knew what presents were coming.

"Sorry about your skis," I said. "I'll pay you back, promise."

"Don't worry about the skis, knuckle brain. What about the jerky, what happened to that?"

"I ate it, every stinky bite."

"Liar, liar, pants on fire."

"Gary!" Becca hissed in disapproval. "Don't talk about fire, okay? Please? Not today."

"What, just because King Man saved us from being crispy critters?"

"Yes, as a matter of fact. Don't be a dolt."

Gronk turned to me. "Dolt? What's a dolt? Oh wait, I'll bet that's a crossword word."

"Hush! It's starting."

At first there was only static. And then, as daylight brightened the windowpanes of the old town hall, the radio crackled to life, and a familiar voice came over the speakers.

You probably know that speech by heart, the one that begins: "My fellow Americans, my fellow citizens, my fellow human beings. We have survived a great darkness, and in the light of dawn we gather not to mourn our dead, but to celebrate the living. We have survived. Whatever is broken, we will fix it together. Whatever has burned, we will build it again. Let us join hands and face the new day. Together we stand, united in purpose, one people made of many . . ."

The speech was repeated every hour for the first couple of days, and school kids will likely have to memorize it for years to come, and do projects on it and stuff. They'll learn to recite the words, but unless you heard it live for the first time, as it was being spoken, you can't really understand what a relief it was to be assured that our country was still there, still standing, and that life would go on.

Nobody knows how many people died when the lights went out. Millions, probably. But more of us survived. They said it would take years to rebuild the power grid and get back to normal, and they're still working on it. Until then, we'll get by with the generosity of our neighbors, and with the help of those who have the courage to rise in defiance of tyranny and ignorance. From the stories people have told and are still telling, Reggie Kingman was far from alone. All across the nation and all around the world, good people helped us find our way.

They shone a light, and the light is love. Remember that and you'll be okay.

EPILOGUE, OR WHAT HAPPENED AFTER THE END

Scientists continue to debate various theories about what caused the normal flow of electrical current to be disrupted after the massive solar event that New Year's Eve. Some cite geomagnetic field interruption, others the effects of a lingering electromagnetic pulse. Thus far there has been no proven or satisfactory explanation for the phenomena, although Mr. Mangano's own particular theory was published in a scientific journal. Whatever the cause, almost all scientists agree it could happen again, and people should be prepared.

Reginald Kingman recovered from his wounds and eventually returned to his old job as school custodian. He continues to be the volunteer police officer for Harmony, New Hampshire, and regularly presides at school assemblies and parades. No one has called him Barf Man in a very long time.

Webster Bragg was indicted for attempted murder of a police officer. He and his family fled their compound with a cache of weapons and a quantity of gold sovereigns. Mr. Bragg remains at large. Rumors that he attempted to establish his own country in the mountains of Paraguay have never been proven.

Mrs. Adler oversaw the rebuilding of the Superette, presided at the grand opening, and then abruptly retired. She intends to run for town council.

Renny Boncoeur and his team of huskies will be competing in the Iditarod next year. His parents, Pete and Louise, plan to be at the finish line in Nome, Alaska.

Much to everyone's surprise, Robert "Boonie" Givens sobered up and got a part-time job. His kids are still bullies and his dogs remain vicious, but there's always hope.

And just last week Rebecca Cobb and Gary "Gronk" Small announced they would be taking each other to the Harmony Harvest & Homecoming Dance.

Charlie is not sure how he feels about that.

FOR THOSE WHO ARE CURIOUS

In 1859 an amateur astronomer named Richard Carrington happened to witness the eruption of a giant fireball from the sun. The resulting collision of the solar flare with Earth's atmosphere caused auroras as bright as daylight. The eruption of the Carrington solar flares was equivalent to the energy of ten billion atomic bombs, and the resulting geomagnetic storm damaged equipment and made it impossible to transmit telegraph signals, the only means of electrical communication at the time.

A similar event today (or tomorrow) might well result in a massive power outage. An even larger event—always a possibility—could be as devastating as the events described in this book.

Try entering the following phrases in a search engine:
Carrington event 1859
Massive solar flare
Coronal mass ejection
Geomagnetic event
Geomagnetic field excursions
Laschamp event
Building a simple crystal radio

Keep reading. Record your thoughts and reactions. And you might want to write it down on paper or print out a copy. Just in case.

ABOUT RODMAN PHILBRICK

Newbery Honor author Rodman Philbrick has written more than a dozen novels for young readers. In 1993, he published his first children's book, *Freak the Mighty*, which became an instant classic and won the California Young Reader Medal, among its many awards. *Freak the Mighty* was also made into a Miramax feature film, *The Mighty*, starring Sharon Stone.

In 2009, Philbrick published a dramatic historical novel about an orphan boy's adventures as he searches for his brother during the Civil War. Filled with colorful detail, as well as the highly emotional role of Maine soldiers during the Battle of Gettysburg, that book, *The Mostly True Adventures of Homer P. Figg*, was chosen as a Newbery Honor Book and an ALA Notable Book.

Philbrick's novels have been received with great acclaim, and they include *Max the Mighty*; *The Fire Pony*; *The Young Man and the Sea*; *REM World*; *The Last Book in the Universe*; and most recently *Zane and the Hurricane: A Story of Katrina*, published in 2014 to numerous starred reviews and citations.

Rodman Philbrick grew up in a small town in New England, and he currently divides his time between Maine and the Florida Keys. You can learn more about him on his website: www.RodmanPhilbrick.com.